'How dare you!'

Nick was silent for several seconds, then he slowly shook his head. 'Oh, I dare, Emma,' he mocked gently.

'Let me go,' she whispered furiously.

'Really, *cara*,' he reproved in a hateful drawl, 'I fail to comprehend a reason for such anger.'

'Next you'll tell me your intentions are strictly honourable, I suppose?' She was so consumed with antipathy that her whole body was beginning to shake with it.

'Are you so sure they are not?'

Her eyes widened, dilating with confusion and, conscious of the painful thudding of her heart, she forced herself to breathe slowly in an effort to gain some measure of control.

'If this is a game,' she indicated unsteadily, 'I don't want to play.'

'Afraid I might win?'

AN AWAKENING DESIRE

BY

HELEN BIANCHIN

MILLS & BOON LIMITED
ETON HOUSE   18–24 PARADISE ROAD
RICHMOND   SURREY   TW9 1SR

First published in Great Britain 1987 by Mills & Boon Limited

© Helen Bianchin 1987

Australian copyright 1987 Philippine copyright 1987 This edition 1987

ISBN 0 263 75845 1

Set in Baskerville 10½ on 11½ pt. 01-1287-47649

Computer typeset by SB Datagraphics, Colchester, Essex

Printed and bound in Great Britain by Collins, Glasgow

For Danilo, Angelo and Peter

CHAPTER ONE

'DARLING, are you quite sure about this trip?'

Emma secured the lock on the expensive piece of luggage and bit back a strangled sound as a tiny hysterical laugh rose and died in her throat. She wasn't *sure* about anything, much less flying half-way across the world, but indecision at this late stage was impossible.

A wry smile tugged at the corners of her generously curved mouth. Maternal devotion could prove daunting, especially when its entire gamut was focused on one sibling.

'I'm twenty-four, not seventeen,' she reminded her mother gently, and Mrs. Templeton lifted a hand only to let it fall again in a gesture of helpless self-defeat.

'If you'd waited, we could have taken a holiday together, Hawaii, Hong Kong—anywhere.'

Which was precisely the reason Emma had insisted on taking a break *now*. The need to get away on her own had become increasingly necessary over the past few months as familial solicitude threatened to destroy each renewed attempt at independence.

Emma refrained from commenting as she crossed to the dressing-table to add the finishing touches to her make-up. Via mirrored reflection she glimpsed the anxiety clouding her mother's attractive features, and for a brief second she was consumed with guilt.

Damn! Why did leaving have to prove so difficult? Her

lipstick slipped, and she plucked a tissue from its nearby box with shaking fingers.

'It's only a year since——' Mrs Templeton's voice faltered to an awkward halt, and Emma finished quietly,

'Since Marc died.' Her eyes captured her mother's and held them with a steadiness that was uncontrived. 'Believe me, I won't go to pieces if you say it.'

There was a measurable silence, one she didn't attempt to fill as she finished outlining her mouth. Mascara came next, and she applied the brushed wand to her lashes with skill before capping and tossing it among the array of cosmetics in her make-up pouch.

'Your father and I are concerned you're attempting too much, too soon.'

Oh, lord, what could she say? Admit her mother was voicing her own uncertainties? No, she reflected wearily. For both their sakes, she had to project enthusiasm. Anything less would be intolerable. 'Three weeks is hardly a lifetime,' she chided gently.

Standing back from the mirror, she viewed her image with critical appraisal, studying the dark auburn curls with something akin to resignation. Reaching her shoulders, the tapered length of her hair was an encumbrance she'd learnt to bear with over the years. Expensive experiments by a number of hair designers had elicited the unanimous opinion she should retain her natural curls, and for the past seven years she'd opted for a casual windswept style which served to highlight her delicately boned features.

Of average height and fashionably slim, she bore feminine curves in all the right places. Tawny-coloured eyes were set wide apart above a *retroussée* nose and a soft, curved mouth. Identical dimples deepened whenever she smiled, alluding to a captivating personality whose warm spontaneity was totally without guile.

Selecting something suitable to wear for the long flight had afforded more than scant deliberation, and she viewed the emerald-green dress in uncrushable silk with approval. Elegant, slim-heeled black shoes completed the outfit, and her only jewellery—aside from her wedding ring—was a gold roped chain and matching bracelet. The overall effect portrayed designer *élan* at its most chic.

Emma fastened her make-up pouch and slipped it into her overnight bag, checked her travel documents, then she slid her arms into a fine wool coat that was light, yet warm, and could be discarded on arrival in Rome.

'Shall we go?'

It would take thirty minutes to reach Sydney's International Air Terminal, and a further half-hour to check in her luggage and attend to formalities.

However, two delayed flights resulted in the passenger lounge being overcrowded, and Emma felt as awkward as her parents did, uttering inanities that had little perspective and merely served to compound her own insecurity.

'I'll send you a postcard every few days,' she promised with a shaky smile as the threat of tears added impetus to the need for a swiftly taken farewell.

Once past the security barrier and out of their sight she was able to regain a measure of control, although her emotions seemed caught up in an unenviable tangle, conversely urging her to *stay* now that she was actually going.

A hollow laugh rose up in her throat as she joined the queue of passengers waiting to complete the electronic check of hand-luggage prior to boarding the huge

Boeing. If she didn't summon some semblance of inner calm, she'd soon be reduced to a quivering mass of nerves!

Her designated seat was next to a window, and as soon as they were airborne she ordered a vermouth and soda, glad of its relaxing effect as she gazed sightlessly at the pale grey sky with its heavy banks of slow-moving cloud.

Despite a determination not to lapse into retrospection, it was all too easy to recall a multitude of bitter-sweet memories centred around one painful figure.

Dear, sweet Marc. Loquacious, fun-loving, endearing. Why *you*? she demanded silently.

Two of Sydney's élite families, the marriage of the year between respective only children, their future had promised so much. A fatal car accident a mere week after their wedding had robbed her of childhood sweetheart, husband and lover, in one brutal swoop, whereas she had been pulled from the passenger seat virtually unscathed apart from some lacerations, two cracked ribs and severe bruising.

After her release from hospital and necessary convalescence, her work as a fashion co-ordinator to an exclusive designer became all-important, and during the ensuing months she devoted long, hard hours in an effort to dull the edges of an inconsolable loss.

It hadn't needed a physician to point out the telltale signs of exhaustion, both mental and physical. His cautioning merely aided her decision to get away from loving, over-protective parents and parents-in-law, as well as a cluster of well-meaning friends whose combined solicitude enveloped her like a shroud, almost to a point whereby she thought she might suffocate from so much caring attention.

'Please fasten your seat-belt.'

The hostess's smooth reminder jolted Emma out of her reverie, and she automatically attended to the clasp as the Boeing began its descent towards Melbourne's Tullamarine Airport, the last Australian port and the shortest of three scheduled stop-overs.

The adjacent seat became occupied by a sweet-faced woman of middle years who regaled Emma with the life history of her five children and four grandchildren all the way to Singapore where she disembarked, and Emma took the opportunity while the jet was stationary to stretch her legs and freshen up. She felt tired and had the vague beginnings of a headache. With luck, the seat next to her would remain empty. If not, she'd feign sleep all the way to Bombay!

Fate elected to be unkind, and she cursed beneath her breath as a tall, masculine frame eased itself down beside her just prior to take-off.

Perhaps if she immersed herself in a magazine he would correctly assume her disinterest in indulging in polite conversation and leave her alone? With that thought in mind she reached into her overnight bag, selected one of three glossy magazines, and began studiously leafing through its pages.

After a while her attention wandered, drawn as if by some elusive magnet to the man at her side, dispassion-ately noting the quality and cut of his dark grey business suit. The faint aroma of his aftershave teased her nostrils—Yves St Laurent's *Kouras*, she identified, reluc-tantly approving his choice. A gold Rolex graced his wrist, and she saw that his hands were broad with strong, tapering fingers and clean square-cut nails.

A man who spent his time jetting between one country

and another, closing corporate deals? Emma mused speculatively, assessing his age to be in the vicinity of mid-to-late thirties. He extracted a folder from his briefcase and became engrossed for the next few hours with an impressive sheaf of papers. Perhaps a member of one of the accepted professions embarking on a conference? Somehow he looked more like a high-powered executive—in control, rather than beneath directorial domination.

A faint smile lifted the edges of her lips. People-watching could be an absorbing pastime, allowing one's imagination to weave a fantasy that was in all probability the antithesis of reality.

Choosing another magazine she selected an article and read it, then another, before settling for an unconventional short story which proved interesting, if a trifle avant-garde for her taste.

She must have dozed, for she came sharply awake at the faint thudding sound of the jet's wheels touching down on the runway, followed within minutes by the discovery that her seat-belt had been fastened while she slept. By whom? The man at her side? Somehow the fact that he'd reached across and calmly tended to the task without her being aware of it was vaguely disturbing.

The need to freshen up elicited a murmured request to slip past him, and as he stood to his feet and moved into the aisle she registered that even in three-inch heels her eyes were barely level with the impeccable knot of his dark silk tie.

Emma's cool 'Thanks' evoked a vaguely mocking smile, and in those few seconds she was made aware of strong, arresting features: a composite of chiselled bone-structure and smooth tanned skin, dark, well groomed hair, and a pair of wide-set, piercing brown eyes.

Ten minutes later she resumed her seat, relieved that this was the final stop-over. It brought her destination closer, despite the sad reminder that Marc should have been sharing this trip as a celebration of their first wedding anniversary. Now she was doing it alone, and she hadn't been able to explain to anyone precisely *why*.

'A pleasure trip?'

At the sound of that deep, slightly accented drawl Emma schooled her expression into a polite mask, not really wanting to converse with him at all; and she glimpsed his lips twist into the semblance of a smile as she accorded him a faint nod in silent acquiescence.

'I shan't eat you.'

He sounded *amused*, and it rankled unbearably. With considerable coolness she let her eyes sweep his features in deliberate appraisal. 'Whatever makes you think I'd allow it?' she inclined with arctic civility, her dismissal containing such crystal clarity that only the most audacious male would have dared pursue another word.

His gaze was assessing beneath its indolent veneer, yet strangely watchful, almost as if he sensed an acute vulnerability beneath her icy façade, and after seemingly endless seconds her lashes slowly fluttered down as her ability to out-stare him diminished.

A prickle of unease slithered the length of her spine, and she shivered, instinctively aware that he was the sort of man who commanded most women at will, and took pleasure in every sensual pursuit.

Perhaps if she adjusted her seat and leaned back against the cushioned head-rest she might manage to escape into sleep. Surely she should be able to? Her body clock was attuned to another time sequence, and she closed her eyes in the hope of drifting into blessed oblivion.

The touch of a hand on her arm caused her to stir, and she blinked, disorientated for a few seconds by her surroundings. Then she became humiliatingly aware that her head was resting against a hard, muscular shoulder!

She moved at once, conscious of a faint tinge of pink colouring her cheeks as her fingers sought the appropriate button to restore the seat to an upright position.

'I'm sorry.' The words emerged scarcely before she could give them thought, and she felt flustered and curiously fragile. *Why*, for God's sake? The man was a stranger, and the chance of them meeting again had to be in the vicinity of one in a thousand.

'Whatever for?' His voice held quiet mockery, and to Emma's ears it sounded impossibly cynical.

Perhaps he was so used to women flinging themselves at him, using every known ruse, that he thought she was merely trying to gain his attention.

Deep inside a tiny seed of resentment flared into antagonism, and for the remainder of the flight she alternately read, became lost in reflective thought, and obviously slept, for when she woke the sky beyond the window was tinged with the first opalescent glow of a new day's dawn, and she watched in idle fascination as the deep blue gradually lightened, casting a pale, eerie illumination of the jet's silver-metalled wing.

Breakfast was served an hour before their scheduled arrival in Rome, and Emma eyed the array of food with uninterest, selecting a croissant which she broke in half and spread with apricot conserve. After drinking a second cup of coffee she silently admitted to feeling almost human.

Disembarkation at Fiumicino International Airport and dealing with Customs took considerable time. There was a brief glimpse of her companion's tall frame as he joined a separate queue, then when next she glanced into the bustling crowd he was no longer in sight.

At last she was free to emerge into the Arrival Lounge with her luggage, and she stood searching for a familiar face in the sea of waiting people, wondering whether Marc's grandparents would come to meet her themselves or despatch their chauffeur.

'*Emma!*'

She might be in a strange city—*country*, she amended silently—but the elderly man threading his way towards her was endearingly familiar. For as long as she could remember, Marc's grandparents had regularly flown to Sydney each year to spend Christmas with their son and his family.

'*Cara!* It is so good to see you.'

'And you,' Emma greeted shakily, blinking quickly as she became enveloped in his embrace.

'Come, the car is outside,' Enzo Martinero bade, taking charge of the luggage trolley, and she walked at his side to a large saloon car parked at the kerb, with a chauffeur at the wheel.

The air was hot and dry, and filled with a cacophony of sound. Jarring hornblasts as taxis jostled with privately driven vehicles for space; voices raised in voluble Italian, altercations which, if Emma's reasonable command of the language proved correct, questioned parentage and managed to blaspheme the Deity with formidable disregard.

Within minutes her luggage was stored and, seated in the rear beside Marc's grandfather, Emma watched as the chauffeur eased the car clear of immediate traffic.

This was *Rome*! Where great emperors had ruled and been defeated, she mused, and ancient civilisation dated back to the years before the birth of Christ. Little wonder they called it the Eternal City.

'Rosa would have accompanied me to meet you, but Annalisa, our young guest, was not feeling well when she woke this morning.' A smile creased Marc's grandfather's kindly features. 'The result of too much excitement, I think.' As if he sensed her curiosity, he sought to elaborate. 'Annalisa is the daughter of our nephew and godson.' He paused fractionally and gave a slight, philosophical shrug. 'Each year Annalisa travels from Milan with her governess to spend the summer holidays with us.'

Emma was intrigued. 'How old is she?'

'Nine. Nick is a devoted father,' Enzo hastened to assure as he caught her perplexed frown. 'Unfortunately his business interests demand much of his time, hence Annalisa attends a boarding school run by the good Catholic Sisters.'

Emma conjured up a picture of a child trapped in a strict scholastic regime, and felt her interest quicken. 'Surely a governess is superfluous?'

They were skirting the city, their progress often slowing to a complete standstill in heavily congested traffic, and although Enzo's luxurious vehicle was air-conditioned the outside noise filtered through the closed window, punctuating their conversation with frequent blasts on the horn by a host of impatient drivers.

'Perhaps governess is the incorrect term,' he declared

with thoughtful contemplation. 'Silvana Delrosso is many things. A distant cousin related to Nick by marriage, she is tutor, companion; the one woman constant in Annalisa's life since the death of her mother.'

'I see.' Did she? Silvana could be a martinet or an angel.

'Nick arrives tomorrow. I am sure you will get on well together.'

Heavens, she didn't know whether to be pleased or dismayed at the prospect. 'You should have said you were expecting guests,' she demurred, unsure now if her visit was convenient.

'Nonsense,' the older man reiterated at once, his pleasant features creasing with genuine concern. 'We are overjoyed for you to be here. Our home is large, with many rooms.' He reached out and took hold of her hand, enfolding it within his own. 'You must not think for one minute, one *second*, that your visit is ill-timed. We adore to have family around us.' His expressive eyes were eloquent in their sincerity. 'And you, sweet Emma, are special. You are the wife of our only grandson.'

She felt a lump rise in her throat, and she swallowed it convulsively. Then she leant forward and brushed her lips against his weathered cheek. 'Thank you.'

CHAPTER TWO

THE Martinero villa was large, nestling high against one
of the many rolling hills that encompassed Tivoli. Set in
spacious grounds and commanding a spectacular view,
its neo-classical exterior had become mellowed with age.
Scrupulously tended gardens, blooms ablaze with riotous
colour abounded within symmetrical borders and sat like
semi-precious gems against a green, velvet smooth-lawn.
Shrubs were clipped with expert precision to retain a
conic shape, and a fountain, complete with statuary and
cascading water, graced the circular courtyard.

Emma slid out from the car and stood hesitantly as
Enzo crossed round to her side, then together they moved
forward and mounted the few steps leading to the main
entrance.

Almost at once the solid double doors were flung open
and she found herself drawn into a warm, welcoming
embrace by Marc's grandmother.

Elegantly slim, Rosa Martinero possessed a sparkling
vivacity that belied her age. 'Emma. Let me look at you.'

Held at arm's length for a few seconds, there was little
Emma could do but offer a tremulous smile as kindly
brown eyes searched her features in caring appraisal.

'I cannot believe you are actually here.' Rosa shook
her head slightly and gave Emma an affectionate hug.
'And you are even more thin than when we last saw you.'
She lifted a hand and lightly traced Emma's cheek.

18

'Come inside, my dear. It has been a long flight, hmm? Accustomed as I am to them, they are incredibly wearing. You will want to shower and change.'

The foyer was magnificent. Marble floors, cool painted walls displaying several exquisite works of art, and a central double staircase provided an impressive backdrop for a white three-tiered fountain, above which a sparkling crystal chandelier hung suspended in dazzling splendour.

'I have put you in the eastern wing,' Rosa conveyed as she led the way upstairs. 'It has a lovely aspect, and I am sure you will be comfortable there.'

'You have a beautiful home,' Emma declared sincerely as she was ushered into a generously proportioned room furnished with gracious rosewood pieces. A large four-poster bed was a focal point, furbished with dusky pink brocade, satin and lace. It was delightfully feminine and bore a slight air of granduer.

'Thank you, *cara*.' A twinkle gleamed in the older woman's eyes as she indicated a door to Emma's left. 'The villa may be old, but we have modern plumbing. Each guest room has its own bathroom.' She turned at the sound of a discreet knock on the outer door. 'Ah, here is Carlo with your luggage. Maria will unpack while you bathe, and afterwards you must come down to the *sala*. Lunch will be served in an hour.'

Alone, Emma extracted toiletries and fresh under-wear, then she made her way into the adjoining bathroom. Sheer luxury, she decided as she filled the capacious spa-bath, adding bath oil with a delicate floral fragrance. It would be all too easy to close her eyes and drift into blissful sleep, letting the gently pulsing water soothe her tired body.

Fifteen mintues later she emerged into the bedroom with a towel fastened sarong-wise around her slim curves to discover the contents of her luggage reposing neatly on hangers in the wardrobe and in drawers of the delicately carved rosewood dressing-table.

Of Maria there was no sign, and Emma quickly donned clean underwear, then she selected a pale blue silk dress with a swirling skirt of tiny pleats and slipped it over her head, securing the zip fastener with ease. Sleeveless, it looked cool and fresh and showed her fine-textured skin to advantage. Make-up was kept to a minimum, and after pulling a brush through her hair she stood back, well pleased with her mirrored reflection.

A swift glance at her watch revealed it had been over half an hour since she'd begun her ablutions, and, stifling the sensation she should be retiring rather than dining, she turned and left the room.

It seemed for ever since she'd last slept in a bed, and as for *sleep*—a few hours of intermittent dozing aboard the plane could scarcely be termed adequate rest.

'Ah, there you are, my dear. I was just coming to fetch you.' Rosa's smile gentled as she slipped a hand through the younger girl's arm. 'I expect you could do with a drink. Enzo is waiting for us in the *sala* with Annalisa and Silvana.'

Together they descended the curving staircase and moved along a wide hallway whose walls were studded with beautiful tapestries.

Situated on the southern side of the villa, the *sala* was a large room with high ceilings and several french doors opening out on to a wide, balustraded terrace from which steps led down to a rectangular-shaped swimming pool. From this distance the tiled depths looked infinitely cool and inviting, Emma decided wistfully as she dragged her eyes back to the room. Casually furnished, it bore a light airiness that was enhanced by ceramic urns containing masses of leafy green foliage and indoor flowering plants.

'Emma, allow me to introduce you to my great-niece, Annalisa. And her governess, Silvana Delrosso.'

Dear heaven, the child was exquisite! A Botticelli angel! Emma smiled and gravely took the small hand extended in formal greeting.

'I am very pleased to meet you.'

'Hello, Annalisa.' Her voice held genuine warmth as she met solemn interest reflected in a pair of unblinking hazel eyes. The young girl looked more suitably dressed to model a junior *Miss Pears* soap commercial than to greet a distant relative all the way from Australia.

Dragging her eyes away, she met the carefully schooled features of the child's tutor and proffered a polite smile.

'Silvana.'

'Signora Martinero.'

Oh dear, she sounded rather austere, Emma decided involuntarily, wondering why Silvana insisted on formality when she looked to be only in her early thirties.

'Oh, please,' she demurred out loud, 'call me Emma.' Her smile widened as she glanced towards Rosa. '*Two* Signora Martineros in the same household can only lead to confusion.'

'May I call you Emma, too?' a young voice queried, and Emma was about to agree when Rosa inclined with accustomed gentleness,

'*Piccina*, I think it must be *zia*, yes?'

'But *you* are my *zia*,' Annalisa declared seriously.

'Cannot it be Zia Rosa, and Zia Emma?' Enzo suggested quizzically, and was the recipient of a solemn unwavering gaze.

'If you say so, *Zio*.'

Enzo leant forward and lightly touched the young girl's cheek. 'Perhaps we can let your *papa* decide, hmm?' He straightened and moved towards a lacquered cabinet. 'Now that everyone is here, we shall have some wine.'

Emma accepted a crystal goblet filled with Moselle and sipped it slowly, aware that its effect could be potent combined with jet-lag.

Lunch comprised a beef consommé, followed by a selection of cold meats and varied salads served with crunchy bread rolls, and a *compote* of fresh fruit for dessert. Emma sipped iced water between each course and joined in the conversation, becoming vaguely fascinated by Annalisa's exceptionally good manners. Behaviour so faultless in such a young child was laudable, but Emma couldn't help feeling it would have been more natural to glimpse a slight lack of restraint, although the reason was self-evident when, at the end of the meal, the young girl folded her napkin carefully and replaced it on to the table before politely requesting to be excused.

'Make ready for your siesta, Annalisa,' Silvana instructed with quiet authority.

'*Si*, Silvana.'

'*Yes*,' the governess corrected. 'It is luncheon, Annalisa. During which we speak English, do we not?'

'Yes, Silvana.'

Emma experienced a mixture of mild irritation and

barely contained surprise as she hastened to assure gently, 'You mustn't feel obliged to speak English solely for my benefit. My command of Italian is reasonably fluent.' Her eyes softened as she met Annalisa's solemn gaze. 'Do you learn English at school?' she queried with genuine interest. 'You speak it very well.'

'No, Zia Emma. We begin English next year. It is *Papa* who insists I must speak English and French. To practise, I speak French at breakfast, English at lunch, and Italian at dinner.' The round hazel eyes widened even further. 'Do you speak French?'

For heaven's sake! Annalisa's father and Silvana Delrosso would make a good pair, she decided wryly. 'I am able to comprehend a fairly extensive menu written in French,' she declared with a deprecatory shrug, then added with a smile, 'I shall have to be silent at breakfast, and only offer a Gallic *non* or *oui*—hopefully in the right places.'

Annalisa blinked twice, then offered with the utmost politeness. 'I could help you learn, if you would like to.'

Why, in the name of several sacred saints, did the child have to have lessons during the holidays? 'Thank you,' she acknowledged, not daring to glance at Rosa or Enzo. 'It's very kind of you, but I'd prefer to brush up on my Italian than attempt to learn a third language.'

'You may speak with Mrs Martinero tomorrow, Annalisa,' Silvana reproved firmly. 'Please go to your room.'

Emma felt her eyes drawn to the small, dark-blonde-haired figure, watching as the young girl obediently excused herself and walked from the room.

There was something poignantly *lonely* about the

child—never alone. Who, after all, she decided with a hint of cynicism, could be *alone* in a house filled with servants and doting relatives?

Unconsciously her eyes slid back to the table, and she glimpsed Rosa's eloquent gaze, then it was masked, and afterwards Emma wondered if she'd imagined it.

'Perhaps you'll excuse me?' She removed her napkin and placed it on the rich damask. 'I'm very tired, and I'd like to rest for a few hours.'

'Of course,' Rosa acceded at once, her kindly expression softening with sympathy. 'You must telephone your parents.' She spared a glance at her watch. 'Just before dinner, I think. Then it will be morning in Australia.'

It was a relief to escape, and when Emma reached her room she closed the door and sank down on to the bed, tired to the point of exhaustion.

Slipping off her shoes, she eased the counterpane to one side, then lay down. The pillow was soft, the mattress seeming to mould itself to her slight weight. Her eyes felt weary, almost gritty with tiredness, and she closed them in a gesture of self-defence.

It would be dark and cold in Sydney, the city's streets slick with winter rain. Quite suddenly she wished she was back there, in her parents' home and in her own bed.

When Emma woke there was light filtering through the drapes, a faint stirring of movement as the silken folds parted beneath the slight breeze wafting in through the open window.

Emma blinked slowly, disorientated by her surroundings for a few scant seconds until memory surfaced. Just how long had she been asleep, for heaven's sake?

A knock at her door was immediately followed by entry into the room by a young woman carrying a tray, and Emma looked at her with dawning dismay. It couldn't be *morning*, surely?

'*Buon giorno, signora.*'

A hollow groan left Emma's lips as she struggled into a sitting positon and took the tray.

'Zia Emma? May I come in?'

A smile widened Emma's generous mouth as she caught sight of Annalisa standing anxiously just inside the doorway. 'Of course.' The little girl looked perfectly groomed from head to toe, her gleaming hair caught with a ribbon each side of her face.

'Zia Rosa said I could come and tell you that breakfast will be ready in an hour.' Her forehead creased with earnestness at the importance of her mission. 'We thought you would be hungry, so that is why Maria has brought croissants to have with your coffee.'

'*Scusi, signora.*' Maria poured steaming, aromatic liquid into a cup, then moved quickly from the room.

Croissants and a choice of three fruit conserves. Emma broke one and spread it with plum jam, then took an appreciative sip of coffee. Absolutely delicious.

'Will you have some with me?' She proffered a portion to Annalisa, who looked doubtfully unsure. 'One mouthful won't spoil your appetite.'

'*Papa——*'

'Isn't here to object,' Emma declared quietly. The more she thought about Annalisa's father, the more she was disinclined to meet him. An austere businessman too immersed in financial pursuits to bother about his daughter wasn't an appealing prospect.

'*Papa*,' Annalisa persisted hesitantly, moving a step further towards the side of the bed, 'and I often share breakfast together when I am not in school.' Her eyes were incredibly solemn. 'Sometimes,' she paused, as if imparting a secret, lowering her voice until it was scarcely more than a whisper, '*Papa* gives Silvana the day off, and we go on a picnic.'

'Really?' Emma tried hard not to smile at such a revelation, for the vision of father and daughter indulging in such frivolity was difficult to comprehend. 'That sounds like fun.' She broke off the end of a croisssant and spread it with strawberry jam, then offered it to the young girl. 'If I eat any more, I won't have room for breakfast.' Pushing the near-empty plate to one side, she sipped what remained of her coffee.

'You will want to shower and dress,' Annalisa stated, taking a few backward steps, and Emma nodded in silent agreement.

'I won't be long.'

As soon as the door closed she pushed the covers aside and slid from the bed. In the adjoining bathroom she reached into the shower recess and turned both crystal knobs, then she quickly slipped out of her dress and stepped beneath the warm spray of water.

Twenty minutes later she was dressed in a pale honey-coloured sleeveless dress with a scooped neckline and slim-fitting skirt. A wide leather belt skimmed the top of her hips, accentuating her small waist, and she slid her feet into low-heeled soft leather sandals before crossing to the dressing-table to tug a brush through her hair in an attempt to restore some kind of order to the curling tresses. Making-up came last, and she patted a light dusting of powder over a thin film of moisturiser, added a touch of clear pink gloss to her lips, then she turned and left the room.

Despite the relatively early hour, the heat of the sun was beginning to make itself felt as it streamed in through the high-sashed windows and open french doors, fingering the marble floors with bright, geometrically patterned light.

Various beautiful antique pieces bore a rich patina from years of loving care, and there were freshly cut flowers arranged in numerous vases at every turn.

Emma's footsteps slowed almost to a halt as she admired the soft-brushed pastels of a misty Monet, and an equally superb Renoir nearby.

'You are interested in art, *signora*?'

She turned slightly at the sound of a feminine voice and met Silvana's carefully assembled features.

'From a purely aesthetic viewpoint,' she concurred, wondering why she should sense a faint feeling of antagonism emanating from Annalisa's governess. Surely it had to be the result of her overly sensitive imagination?

'I favour Picasso, or the tortured Van Gogh. So much brilliance and flair.'

It depended whether she meant the former at his conventional or flamboyant best, and Emma merely inclined her head in silent acknowledgement.

'I believe Signora Martinero has instructed breakfast to be served on the terrace.'

Minutes later Emma walked through wide-open french doors leading from the *sala* and was greeted with hearty enthusiasm by Enzo, followed by a warmly affectionate hug from Rosa.

'You slept well? Ah, let me look at you. Yes, better, much better.' Enzo pulled out a chair and motioned her to take a seat. 'Orange juice?'

He filled a glass and handed it to her, then resumed his position at the head of the table, content to leave the serving of food to Rosa.

Numerous covered platters reposed on a mobile trolley, together with a steaming pot of coffee, and after refusing a variety of tempting hot dishes Emma settled for a small serving of muesli, followed by toast and coffee.

Silvana studiously monitored Annalisa's fare, insisting on a nutritional balance with muesli, soft-boiled egg and toast, together with a glass of milk.

'It is a beautiful day, so warm already,' Rosa intimated with a charming smile. 'After breakfast you might like to use the pool.' Her gaze shifted towards Annalisa, and her eyes softened. 'Perhaps you could entertain Zia Emma this morning. Would you like that?'

'Oh, *yes!*' The young girl's elated agreement made Emma smile. 'If Silvana has nothing planned,' she ventured hesitantly, her expression assuming diffident solemnity.

'Very well, you have my permission.'

Annalisa's eyes shone. 'Thank you.'

'I will be in my room attending to correspondence, if you should need me.' Silvana declared, cautioning her young charge. 'Try not to chatter too much, or bother Mrs Martinero with too many questions.'

'Yes, Silvana,' Annalisa responded meekly, and immediately the governess was safely indoors she finished her milk and sat almost breathlessly still, her hazel eyes round with barely suppressed excitement.

Emma didn't have the heart to dally over a second coffee, and some ten minutes later she traversed the wide steps leading down towards the pool with Annalisa close by her side.

'Tell me what it is like in Australia, Zia Emma. Is it true there are cattle stations with thousands of acres?' Her young face was alive with curiosity.

'Millions,' Emma corrected softly. 'Some are so large it takes several stockmen weeks to inspect boundary fences.'

'Don't they use helicopters?'

'Sometimes. It depends on their financial status. Helicopters and planes used for aerial surveillance are expensive to maintain. Owners often prefer four-wheel-drive vehicles, trail-bikes, or stockmen on horseback.'

'I thought men who owned that much land must be rich!' Annalisa declared, clearly astounded, and Emma laughed.

'Not always. Severe drought can have a disastrous effect, and the farmer must manage to pay for feed and the men's wages. If the drought doesn't abate, as it sometimes doesn't for years, it becomes a vicious circle in the struggle to survive.'

'It doesn't rain for *years*?' Annalisa repeated incredulously.

'Some areas in the Outback haven't seen rain for up to seven years,' she replied solemnly.

'But what happens to all the cattle? So many must die.'

'Australia is a land of many contrasts, where the centre is mostly desert. Dark red sandy soil whose natural vegetation is mainly wild scrub and spinifex.' If she was going to impart an informal geography lesson, she may as well do it properly. 'There are goannas, which look like miniature prehistoric monsters, snakes and lizards, several species of kangaroo, together with the marsupial koala.'

'Where do you live, Zia Emma?'

'In Sydney. While not the capital, it is certainly Australia's largest city,' she explained quietly, aware they had skirted the white-painted balustrading surrounding the pool and were descending a set of stone steps leading down to a terraced garden.

'I have seen pictures of Sydney. It has a large bridge spanning the harbour, lots of tall buildings, and several bays and inlets. It looked pretty.'

'It is,' Emma agreed, visualising the city's landscape without any difficulty at all. 'The harbour is often host to various sailing craft all year round: yachts, cruisers. Most Australians adore the outdoor life—swimming, boating, surfing—sport of one kind or another.'

'Italy is beautiful, too. There are so many places to see,' Annalisa enthused, quite carried away with numerous plans of her own making. '*Papa* telephoned last night from Milan, just before I went to bed. He will be here soon; before lunch, I think.'

A faint fluttering of annoyance stirred deep inside her, then Emma dismissed such a feeling as totally uncharitable. After all, it had been she who had chosen the timing of her visit, not Rosa, and no blame could be attributed to Marc's grandmother. As Enzo had so charmingly pointed out, the villa was large enough to accommodate several guests, and although *she* was family, Rosa's nephew and his daughter were equally family and just as entitled to receive hospitality. Except, if she had known in advance, she would not have come. *Why?* an inner voice demanded. Annalisa is a delightful child, even if Silvana Delrosso appears rather stiff and unfriendly. If the truth be known, it was the imminent appearance of Annalisa's father, Nick—— A faint frown creased her forehead as she realised she didn't even know his surname, and a grimace momentarily twisted her lips. She didn't want to meet any eligible member of the opposite sex, for the simple reason she didn't feel equipped to deal with the consequences when projected charm was met with polite rebuff. The male ego was incredibly fragile, she'd discovered, unable to comprehend why a courteous rejection should elicit on most occasions such wounded reaction.

'I'm sure your *papa* will want a relaxing holiday,' Emma reiterated quietly, unwilling to dampen the young girl's enthusiasm by openly refusing the invitation to be included on any excursions.

'But he does relax,' Annalisa hastened to assure. 'He says to stay in one place and not be for ever boarding planes *is* relaxing—by comparison, that is.'

The vision of a jaded jet-setter sprang immediately to mind, and Emma wasn't sure she liked the projected impression. He probably had a number of mistresses in capital cities throughout the world, she decided dourly, while purporting to be a doting father on his own home ground.

'I think he would prefer to spend as much time with you as possible,' she demurred, only to hear Annalisa reassure quickly,

'But he *will* be with me. We will be together just the same if you are there, too. Except it will be better. Please,

Zia Emma. You will come, won't you?'

Oh dear! To be implored so eagerly was flattering, but nevertheless she was non-committal, tempering her words with a faint smile. 'I'll think about it.'

'If I ask *papa* to invite you, he will,' Annalisa declared with sureness, and Emma's expression assumed a certain wryness.

'And will you tell your father that you have already issued me an invitation, and convey that I might agree?'

The young girl's features became grave as she met Emma's questioning gaze. 'You think I would play each of you against the other in order to get my own way?'

Damn! Why did it have to prove so difficult to opt out of something she instinctively felt might be misconstrued? Seeking a change of subject she inclined an arm towards various statuary gracing the gardens, their symmetry enhanced by a stand of majestic pines. Every statue bore a graceful beauty, despite being weathered with age.

'Do you know whom they each represent?'

'Of course,' Annalisa answered politely. 'Silvanus is the first; he was the mythological god who protected forests, fields and gardens. It must be true, for the gardens here are very beautiful, are they not?'

Emma had to agree as she took in a variety of multi-coloured carefully tended flora. From brilliant reds to palest pink, with splashes of white, grown in beds banked between terraced paths leading down the gentle slope to the southern boundary.

It was hot, the sun's heat seeming to have intensified in the short time since they'd left the villa. With a rueful glance she caught sight of the slightly pink skin on her arms and knew that if she didn't seek the protection of sunscreen cream soon, she'd burn.

'Would you like to join me for a swim?' The thought of slipping into the pool's cool, sparkling depths held infinite appeal, and she was heartened by Annalisa's enthusiastic response.

'I was hoping you would ask. I don't enjoy swimming on my own. It's not nearly as much fun.'

By tacit agreement they turned and retraced their steps indoors, mounting the curved staircase together.

'I'll meet you downstairs in five minutes,' Emma suggested as she reached the door to her bedroom. 'OK?'

'OK.' Annalisa's dark eyes sparkled with anticipatory pleasure. 'I will tell Zia Rosa where we will be.'

In the bedroom Emma moved quickly across the room and pulled open a drawer, extracting a bikini in bright gold synthetic silk before tossing it to one side in search of the one-piece she'd packed on the spur of the moment. A *maillot*, it was simple but daringly cut, and black, flattering her pale skin—milk-white, she amended somewhat wryly several minutes later as she checked her appearance in the mirror. Picking up a short beach jacket, she slipped it on, caught up a towel, then she made her way from the bedroom.

The water was refreshing and deliciously cool, and she surfaced from a neat shallow dive to hear a splash close by as Annalisa followed her lead.

For more than an hour they alternately swam or floated atop body-length rubber cushions. Emma emerged to re-apply sunscreen cream to her body, then she slipped back into the water to leisurely stroke several lengths of the pool, deliberately pacing her own style to match that of Annalisa, who was making an admirable effort to keep up.

'I think I've had enough,' Emma vouched as she reached the pool's edge a few seconds behind her young companion. 'How about you?' She lifted a hand and smoothed water from her hair, wishing now she'd thought to wear an adequate cap instead of the silk scarf she'd tied round her hair.

'It was wonderful,' Annalisa enthused vivaciously, a wide smile almost stretching her mobile mouth from one ear to the other. 'I won! I really beat you, didn't I?' For a moment a faint frown clouded her attractive features. 'You didn't let me win, did you?'

'Now why would I do that?' Emma parried as she placed her hands on to the slate tiles and levered her body up in one fluid movement to sit on the pool's edge. Then she leaned forward and took Annalisa's outstretched hand and pulled her up to sit at her side.

'Because you are taller than me, and your arms are longer,' the young girl declared solemnly, watching with fascination as Emma untied the scarf and released her hair.

It sprang vibrantly free and with a faint grimace she squeezed the excess water out and pushed her fingers through its thickness in an attempt to restore a modicum of order.

'I'm also unfit,' she offered lightly, all too aware of the faint pull of muscles sadly out of tone. It didn't pay to remember that she'd been something of a fitness fanatic, loving to participate in several sports, particularly tennis, netball and aerobics. Marc had been equally avid, and they'd shared work-outs together, revelling in maintaining a physical peak. In the past year she hadn't played a single game of anything, although she'd resorted to gentle yoga exercises, preferring solitude against part-nered competitiveness.

A faint sound alerted her senses, followed by the distinct chink of ice-cubes as a tray was set down on to the table behind them.

'Oh, good,' Annalisa sighed blissfully. 'Maria has brought us something to drink.'

Emma reached for a nearby towel as Annalisa scrambled to her feet, suddenly aware of a slight prickling sensation at the base of her neck as if some sixth sense had extended its antennae and become acutely attuned to an entity she had yet to recognise.

'*Papa! Qui arrivato!*'

The animated excitement in the young girl's welcome was explicit, and Emma registered a deep, slightly accented voice issue an affectionate paternal greeting in response.

She turned slowly, her gaze travelling towards a tall male frame standing several feet distant. Something about the dark slant of his head, his height, was vaguely familiar, and she lifted a hand to shade her eyes from the sum as Annalisa launched herself into his arms.

Aware that an introduction was imminent, Emma slid to her feet and reached for her beach jacket, unsure as she slipped it on why she should suddenly feel so reluctant to meet the man who was gently disentangling himself from his daughter's embrace.

'Zia Emma, this is my *papa*, Nick Castelli.'

Emma felt her eyes widen with shocked disbelief as she met his faintly mocking gaze, and her stomach lurched in sickening unison with the knowledge that the compelling stranger who had shared part of her flight less than thirty-six hours previously and Annalisa's father were one and the same.

CHAPTER THREE

'MR CASTELLI,' Emma acknowledged formally, unwilling to take his outstretched hand.

He was aware of her reluctance, damn him! It was there in his eyes, the faint, challenging gleam that dared she flout convention and refuse.

'I've heard so much about you,' she remarked with distant civility, placing her hand in his for a few brief seconds. The enveloping warmth of his clasp sent a slight charge of electricity tingling through her veins, and she snatched her hand back in angry confusion.

'Indeed?' His voice was silky-smooth beneath its veneer of musing indulgence, and for some unknown reason an icy frisson of fear slid stealthily down the length of her spine.

There was an elemental ruthlessness apparent beneath his sophisticated façade, a latent strength that was impossible to ignore. A man, she perceived with instinctive insight, who knew exactly what he wanted and pursued his objective with single-minded determination.

'Annalisa and Rosa have spoken of you with the highest regard,' Emma continued with deceptive coolness.

Why should she feel so *betrayed*, for God's sake? Because, a tiny voice whispered insidiously inside her brain, it was impossible to believe *chance* had anything to do with a Martinero nephew and a Martinero granddaughter-in-law sharing adjoining seats on the same long intercontinental flight. That was stretching coincidence a bit too far. Yet with whom could she lay the blame? Her parents, Marc's, Rosa? Nick Castelli for his complicity? It was inconceivable he had been unaware of her identity, for there were sufficient family photographs on display in various rooms within the villa, and a framed enlargement of Marc's wedding held pride of place atop a *chiffonier* in the *salone*.

'Should I be flattered?'

Resentment flared briefly as she met his steady gaze and saw the cool, assessing quality apparent, the strangely watchful element that bore distinct resemblance to a jungle animal at prey.

'Familial devotion is second to none,' Emma accorded with seeming lightness as she became aware of Annalisa's intense interest in their exchange.

'And therefore prejudiced,' he alluded with faintly mocking cynicism.

'I wasn't aware that that was what I implied.'

'No?'

Determination was responsible for the slight, almost winsome smile that widened her generous mouth. That, and a refusal to allow him to best her. 'I wouldn't presume to judge, Mr Castelli. I barely know you.'

A dark gleam momentarily lit his eyes, then it was gone. 'Perhaps we could walk back to the villa together. Rosa dispatched me to tell you that lunch will be ready in half an hour, and you will both need to shower and change.'

Emma had, perforce, to measure her steps with his as they moved up through the terraced gardens. Every instinct bade her break into a run and race as fast as her legs would carry her into the villa, up the stairs and into her room away from this man. Preferably, if it were possible, take flight on the first available jet out of Rome!

'*Papa*, what do you think? Should I call Emma, Zia Emma, or just Emma?' Annalisa queried, hurrying her words quickly together before he could answer, her voice sounding incredibly earnest. 'Zia Rosa does not mind, but Silvana says it should be Mrs Martinero.'

'Which does Emma prefer?' Nick Castelli countered, shooting his daughter a musing glance before shifting his attention to the subject of their conversation.

'Oh,' Annalisa hastened, 'Emma says I should ask *you*.'

'I see.' He sounded grave, as if he was giving the matter serious consideration. 'I imagine it should be Emma's decision,' he drawled at last, watching the play of emotions flit briefly across Emma's expressive features.

He would pass the ball into her court, wouldn't he? 'I prefer Emma,' she acceded quietly, although it was an effort to keep her voice steady.

'Oh, *good*,' Annalisa enthused, her face wreathing with a series of delighted smiles. 'These holidays are going to be such fun, are they not, *Papa*? We can take Emma to Naples, and have picnics together.'

Emma had serious doubts about such arrangements, and it was on the tip of her tongue to demur, except she was keenly aware that that was precisely what he expected her to do.

They reached the terrace, and with a murmured excuse she broke away and moved indoors.

In her room she showered and changed into a blue sleeveless dress whose soft, rolled neckline and flared skirt accentuated her slim curves and tiny waist. Make-up was confined to moisturiser and a touch of colour to her lips,

and, despite a vigorous brushing, her hair sprang away
from her head in a mass of wayward curls, affording
Emma a faint grimace as she ran a final check on her
appearance. Slim-heeled sandals in white leather completed the outfit, and with a quick glance at her watch
she smoothed a shaky hand over her hair, then took a
deep breath and made her way downstairs.

Lunch. Emma wasn't even hungry, and she could
easily have existed on a piece of fruit instead of the
beautifully presented three-course meal served in the
sala.

As it was, she dutifully ate the avocado vinaigrette,
forked a few mouthfuls of salad, declined the sliced ham
and cold chicken and refused dessert.

Throughout the meal she became an interested
spectator, aware that the image she'd conjured of a cold
businessman too caught up with corporate wheeling and
dealing to devote much time to his daughter was
unfounded.

If she was honest, she'd *wanted* to find fault, a flaw that
would give her a legitimate reason to dislike the
indomitable man seated diagonally opposite her at the
table.

Not that she needed a specific reason, for he
represented most things Emma disliked in a man. He was
too attractive and far too self-assured, with a degree of
weary cynicism that was vaguely frightening. Dangerous, she amended. He undoubtedly ate little girls for
breakfast! A sudden shiver feathered up from the base of
her spine and she tensed her shoulders in order to
suppress it. Somehow she doubted his penchant for
feminine companions extended to *girls*; sophisticated
socialites well versed in pleasing a man were more likely

to be his style—the type he could love and leave with little or no commitment. To become involved with someone of Nick Castelli's calibre would be akin to attempting to tame a prowling tiger.

Heavens, what on earth was she thinking of? The last thing she needed was to foster imaginative speculation over any man, much less Rosa's and Enzo's formidable nephew. Yet, of its own will, her attention was continually drawn towards him as she became startingly aware of what he could represent to her peace of mind.

Annalisa's presence at the table provided a necessary distraction, for the young girl's pleasure was patently obvious, and even Silvana's occasional faint frown couldn't dampen her enthusiasm.

It was a relief when the last plate was removed, and Emma declined wine in favour of chilled water, sipping it slowly as Annalisa chattered with her father.

'Silvana is pleased with my results at school. Even Sister Margherita said I did very well. Didn't she, Silvana?'

Emma saw Silvana's lips tighten a fraction, then relax into a courteous smile. 'Indeed. However, your written French could do with some improvement, and there are a few factors of English grammar which you have failed to correctly grasp.' She turned her attention to Nick Castelli, and the subtle change in her expression, a softening that was meant to convey the depth of their long association was plainly evident. 'I have taken the responsibility of ensuring Annalisa does a few hours' study each day. I trust this meets with your approval?'

Annalisa appeared to be sitting on the edge of her seat, her expression one of unconscious pleading as she gazed at her father, and Emma waited with interest to see whose side Nick Castelli would take.

'Perhaps we could reach a compromise?' His voice was silky beneath the smile he projected. Smooth, yet denoting a will of tensile steel. 'As Silvana will be vacationing in Venice until the last week of the school holidays, I suggest studying be relegated until then. How does that sound?'

Annalisa clapped her hands together in delight. 'Thank you, *Papa*.'

'An excellent idea,' Rosa approved. 'Don't you think so, Emma?'

Oh lord, why involve me? Emma queried silently. Yet she was aware of Annalisa's intent air of expectancy, an eagerness for Emma to add her approval. 'Yes, of course.' She deliberately refrained from looking at Nick Castelli, although she sensed his gaze and forced her expression to remain serene. It still irked her that he'd known precisely who she was on that long flight, yet had chosen not to introduce himself. And if he had? What would have been her reaction?

'What plans do you have for tomorrow, *Papa*?' Annalisa began, her eyes sparkling with anticipation. 'Emma can come with us, can't she?'

'That would be nice,' Rosa interceded quickly. 'Silvana's flight leaves early in the morning. You could begin exploring the city itself, or take a picnic lunch into the hills. I have a few days planned for Emma, myself. Shopping, a few fashion showings at some of the famous design houses. Annalisa shall accompany us, if she wishes.'

'I shall be delighted for Emma to join us,' Nick drawled.

'How very kind of you, Mr Castelli.'

'Nicolo,' he corrected imperturbably, and she could have sworn there was an indolent gleam apparent in the depths of his eyes. 'My family and friends call me Nick.'

Her lashes swept up with complete lack of guile as she silently appraised his enigmatic expression, and his eyes held hers in mesmeric confusion, daring her to refuse.

For a moment she almost did, then she caught sight of Annalisa's anxious expression and she experienced a twinge of remorse.

'Really, Nick,' Silvana reproved. 'I am sure Mrs Martinero has plans of her own.'

'Why so formal?' He flicked his attention from one to the other and raised a quizzical eyebrow in Emma's direction. 'You can't want to be referred to as Mrs Martinero for the duration of your stay?'

It would be churlish to respond that she wanted to put up an impenetrable barrier and remain aloof from any extended friendship where he was concerned. Then a hollow laugh died in her throat at the mere thought. Nick Castelli would never be any woman's friend. Such an appellation was far too insipid! Somehow she doubted there was a woman alive who could fail to be aware of the powerful magnetism he exuded. And how did he regard his daughter's governess-companion? Were they bound together merely by virtue of being related, however distantly? Somehow she imagined Silvana retained an affection for her employer that wasn't motivated entirely by her position or connection to the family. Yet there was a resignation apparent and a degree of vague irritation, almost as if Silvana recognised she would never be anything to Nick Castelli other than Annalisa's tutor and companion.

'No,' Emma agreed, and incurred a long, level stare from Silvana.

'I am relieved,' Nick drawled.

'Shall we adjourn to the *salone*?' Rosa suggested. 'Then Maria can clear the table.'

It was an excellent excuse to escape, and Emma used it shamelessly. 'Would you mind if I went to my room and rested for an hour or two?' She still felt tired from the long flight, the dramatic climatic change, and the tension Nick Castelli was able to evoke without any seeming effort at all.

'Of course not, my dear. In fact, we always observe an afternoon siesta,' Rosa explained kindly as she stood to her feet and moved away from the table. 'The shops—everything, in fact, even the business sector—close at one, then re-open again at four, usually until eight.' She reached out and touched Emma's arm. 'Come downstairs whenever you feel like it. Dinner isn't until nine.'

A perfectly civil meal, Emma discovered, during which she ate little and allowed herself to be drawn into conversation with Rosa, Enzo and Annalisa. Nick Castelli she largely ignored, except when good manners demanded otherwise, and it was an immeasurable relief to escape to her room and blissful solitude.

'Please come with us, Emma,' Annalisa implored as she polished off the remainder of her toast and then proceeded to empty the milk in her glass. 'After we see Silvana's flight depart, we could go into the city. You could toss a coin into the Trevi Fountain.' Her eyes lit up with pleasure, and her mouth curved into the most beguiling smile. 'I am sure *Papa* would not mind if we visit some of the famous boutiques along the Via Condotti.'

It sounded tempting, although Emma wasn't sure Silvana would approve, or even if Nick Castelli seconded his daughter's invitation.

'I can see Annalisa has nothing less than the grand tour in store for you,' Nick drawled as he poured himself another cup of coffee, and Rosa added her support.

'I think it is a splendid idea.'

She would be perfectly safe, she determined, with Annalisa in tow. Besides, she really did want to explore, and who better to act as her guide than Nick Castelli?

'Thank you,' she acquiesced politely, blithely ignoring Silvana's faint frown.

Two hours later they set out in Nick's car, a sleek Ferrari Mondial, Emma noted with concealed admiration. Annalisa's animated chatter more than made up for any lack on the part of her governess, and Emma concentrated her attention on the passing scenery for the time it took to reach the airport.

After Silvana had departed, Nick steered them, at Annalisa's insistence, to a café for a thirst-quenching drink, then they drove into the city.

Together they walked at a leisurely pace until they reached the base of the Spanish Steps.

'They are French and Italian,' Nick informed as Emma centred her attention on the broad travertine steps. 'Not Spanish at all.'

The baroque staircase was crowded with lounging teenagers, vendors and souvenir-hawkers, and Emma bore their open admiration with vague embarrassment.

'You have gone pink,' Annalisa declared. 'All Italian men express their appreciation of a pretty girl,' she explained with a warm smile. 'You must not think anything of it.'

She felt Nick's light clasp on her elbow, and quelled an initial instinct to withdraw. Perhaps he sensed it, for his fingers tightened fractionally, and every nerve-end in her body quivered into vibrant life.

'There is the *Trinita dei Monte*,' Nick declared, directing her attention to the twin-belfried French church.

He didn't intimidate her, Emma assured herself, at least not in the accepted sense, yet it was almost as if there was a generation of electricity between them, creating its own shockwaves and pitching her into a state of confusion.

They wandered at will along the Via Condotti, where she looked with envy at Gucci's renowned leather emporium and lingered to admire the jewellery displayed in Bulgari's famed store.

She could have spent *days* just browsing, she decided, determined to return when there was more time. Rosa was sure to have included this glamorous area in one of her planned shopping excursions.

Lunch was a leisurely meal eaten in a pleasant *ristorante*, air-conditioned, Emma discovered much to her relief, for her skin felt flushed with the intense heat. Being plunged into a northern hemispheric summer after experiencing a cold winter in southern climes took some adjustment.

'What will you have, Emma?' Annalisa queried, openly delighted to be sharing her father's company. 'I will have pasta, I think. Their spaghetti is very good, isn't it, *Papa*?'

'Indeed it is,' Nick responded easily. 'Some wine,

Emma? Or perhaps you would prefer chilled mineral water?'

Alcohol in the middle of the day would go straight to her head, especially in this heat, and instinct warned she needed every faculty intact to deal with Annalisa's inestimable father!

'Mineral water, please, and a light garden salad.'

They had almost finished when Annalisa spared her father an imploring glance. 'Can we visit the Trevi Fountain this afternoon, *Papa*?'

Nick afforded her an indulgent smile, as with childish simplicity she set about lining up a number of possible outings that would easily take care of several days.

It was obvious they shared a close bond, but Emma suppressed a faint feeling of unease at the thought of spending so much time in Nick's company. Not that she wasn't grateful, she assured herself, just mildly resentful. Apprehensive, a tiny imp taunted.

'Why don't you invite Emma out to dinner tonight, *Papa*? She has come for a holiday, not to stay at the villa every evening.'

'Why not?' Nick responded before Emma had a chance to refuse.

Damn, she cursed silently. How did she get out of this one? Perhaps she could plead exhaustion, or an aversion to the day's heat, and decline?

It was late when they returned to the villa after a pleasant number of hours spent exploring the city's streets and *piazzas*, where, much to Annalisa's expressed delight, they tossed coins into the Trevi Fountain. Something, Annalisa assured fervently, she always did so that she would return next summer for a vacation with her adored Zia Rosa and Zio Enzo.

Nick brought the car to a halt outside the villa's entrance and Emma slid out, a polite few words of thanks hovering on her lips, followed, she determined, by a suitably regretful excuse not to dine with him.

'Will an hour be sufficient for you to shower and change?'

Her eyes flew to meet his, and she realised at once the subtle taunt beneath his query was meant to convey that he knew she intended to opt out if she could.

'Can I help you choose what to wear?' Annalisa begged, and as Emma glanced from father to daughter any words in excuse of the invitation died as she caught sight of the young girl's enthusiasm.

Afterwards Emma could only query her own sanity as she showered and attended to her toilette. Slipping into fresh underwear, she donned a silk wrap, then at the sound of a tentative knock she crossed to the door and welcomed Annalisa into the room.

'This cream frock, I think,' the youngster declared at last, after admiring the classic lines of an expensive Zampatti original. 'It's beautiful.'

'Are you sure?'

Annalisa's head moved in quick averment. 'Yes,' she declared seriously, watching with intense interest as Emma applied the finishing touches to her make-up.

It was fifteen minutes before they descended the staircase and entered the *salone* where Rosa and Enzo were sharing a pre-dinner drink with Nick.

He looked devastating in impeccable evening attire, Emma decided as she declined Enzo's offer of wine.

For some unknown reason she seemed to have developed a heightened sensitivity where he was concerned that confounded even her as she attempted to analyse its cause.

'Shall we leave?'

There was little she could do but bid Rosa and Enzo goodnight and thank Annalisa for her assistance. Except there was a vague flaring of resentment apparent at his high-handedness.

The Ferrari was parked immediately outside the main entrance, and Emma slid into the front seat whilst Nick crossed round the front of the car and slipped in behind the wheel. With a deft flick of his wrist he fired the engine, then eased the vehicle down the long, curving driveway.

As it paused momentarily at the gates he slanted her a dark glance. 'You are annoyed,' he remarked drily.

'At being railroaded into accepting an invitation I never wanted?' Emma parried, thrusting him an arctic glare. 'Did you expect me not to be?'

The car gathered speed with smooth precision, traversing the winding road with ease beneath Nick's competent expertise.

'I had thought you might enjoy seeing some of Rome's nightlife,' he declared silkily.

'*La dolce vita.*' She hadn't meant to sound quite so cynical, and he spared her a look that was infinitely mocking.

'That particular axiom has acquired à rather unsavoury meaning over the years. I had something more——' He paused.

'Refined?' Emma responded archly.

'In mind? You can be assured of it,' Nick declared and she proferred a smile that was a mere facsimile.

'What if I said I was feeling adventurous?'

'Are you?' There was no doubting his meaning, and Emma didn't dare look at him for fear of glimpsing the amusement she felt sure must be evident. Fool, she accorded wryly. Bandying words with Nick Castelli could only prove to be her undoing. Yet she was darned if she'd let him gain the upper hand.

'Not in the way you imply.'

'Pity.' He caught her outraged expression and offered a twisted smile. 'Relax, Emma. All I have in mind is the enjoyment of some fine wine and excellent cuisine in the company of an attractive companion.'

Relax? How could she *relax*, for heaven's sake? As urbane as he appeared, there was an animalistic sense of power beneath the sophisticated veneer, an inherent vitality that was arresting. Unleashed, whether in anger or passion, it would prove a force she felt ill-equipped to deal with.

'Why me?' she queried simply, sparing him a steady glance. 'I don't want to be entertained. I'd be more than happy to remain at the villa. Rosa and Enzo are delightful company.' Once she started, she couldn't stop. 'I'm sure you can't lack—amenable female companionship.'

'You expect me to deny it?'

'Not at all,' she responded evenly. 'I'm puzzled why you should waste your time.'

'With a woman who is the antithesis of amenable, hmm?'

'I don't want you to feel obligated in any way.'

'What gives you that idea?'

'It would be very easy for Rosa and Enzo to ask you to take pity on their grandson's widow,' she said stoically, and unbidden her chin lifted fractionally as she became aware of his deep, probing glance. 'I left Sydney to get away from over-solicitious family protectiveness.' Her eyes darkened with remembered grief. 'Two sets of parents who treated me like a piece of precious Dresden china, watching and analysing every move I made. I thought I was going to suffocate!'

Her outburst was greeted with silence; then, after what seemed an age, he voiced quietly, 'We are almost there.'

Emma took note of her surroundings, and was unable to contain her surprise. 'I thought we were going into the city.'

'I don't remember saying so.' He eased the car off the road and parked it close to a cluster of time-worn buildings. The pavement was filled with tables and chairs, pottery urns overflowing with flowering plants of various hues which, together with bright-checked tablecloths, green and white striped umbrellas, provided a colourful backdrop to what she identified as a small, bustling *trattoria*.

'I thought you would find it amusing to eat here. The food is extremely good, and the atmosphere informal and friendly.'

It was so different from what she had expected. Somehow she'd envisaged Nick Castelli choosing an elegant restaurant where the city's social echelon wined and dined in sartorial splendour.

'The chef excels with pasta—his *pasta al forno* cannot be bettered anywhere.' He slid out of the car and crossed round to open Emma's door, reaching forward to take hold of her arm as she stood to her feet.

Although it was quite early by Roman standards, there were several patrons seated and she was acutely conscious of their scutiny as she allowed Nick to lead her towards an empty table.

'They are admiring your hair and pale complexion,' Nick murmured with a faint smile, and her lashes lowered in a gesture of self-defence, aware that she provided a startling contrast to the tall, dark-haired man at her side.

'Would you like some wine? Or perhaps you'd prefer a *chinotto*?' he asked as soon as they were seated.

Emma chose the latter, for it was an innocuous beverage, not unlike Coca Cola, and very palatable. The chatter of voices mingled with music emitting from nearby stereo speakers, conspiring to provide a relaxing atmosphere.

'We should have brought Annalisa. She would have enjoyed it.'

His dark, gleaming gaze rested on her expressive features, and a smile tugged the edges of his mouth. 'Yes. However, my daughter considered I deserved to have you to myself.'

What would he say if she revealed she'd prefer Annalisa's company to his? Or at least be able to utilise the young girl's presense as a protective buffer. Sagely she declined to comment, and when they were each handed a menu she took time to study the selections and eventually ordered *pasta al forno* as a starter—only because she enjoyed it, she assured herself firmly, and not due to any recommendation Nick had accorded the dish. Electing to follow it with an individual tossed green salad, she declined dessert.

Nick joined her with the starter, decided on veal *parmigiana* as the main course, and opted for the cheese board.

Emma watched him surreptitiously as he took a measured sip of his wine, and wondered at her sudden lack of *savoir-faire*. There was something vaguely threatening about her companion, a quality she couldn't quite pin down, and it bothered her more than she was prepared to admit. Consequently she felt ill at ease and slightly on edge. There was no recollection, ever, of having been so acutely aware of a member of the opposite sex. It made her feel breathless, heightening the reality by monitoring every single breath she took, which was crazy. The act of breathing was an automatic reflex, for heaven's sake!

'You live in Milan, I believe.' The words were a civil attempt at conversation, a need to say something to fill an empty void, and it irked her that he knew she felt gauche in his company.

'My business interests are centred there.' A slight smile curved his sensuously moulded mouth, and one eyebrow slanted in quizzical amusement. 'Would you like a résumé of my life-style? It might save me answering endless questions.'

Her eyes widened slightly, and a delicate pink tinged her cheeks. 'It wasn't my intention to pry.'

'But you feel vaguely uneasy in my presence,' he persisted musingly. 'And aware of the need to indulge in polite conversation.'

There was a measurable silence, during which she fought to regain her composure, and she viewed the waiter's appearance with relief, glad to have something to do with her hands as she picked up her fork and began to eat.

'You speak English with very little accent at all,' Emma commented, more as an observation that from the need to determine the reason why.

'The result of a comprehensive education,' Nick told her lazily. 'I studied at universities in Milan and London.'

That would account for it, she allowed silently. 'I see.'

'Do you, Emma?' His smile held an element of mockery, and she looked at him carefully.

'What do you want me to say?' she replied quietly, hating his verbal thrust and parry.

'My business interests take me all over the world,' he enlightened her with a certain wryness. 'Despite the rapid advancement of electronic technology in assessing and relaying relevant data, there remains the necessity for personal negotiation.'

'And while you are flitting from one continent to another, Annalisa is well cared for in an educational institution during semesters and she has Silvana to fall back on in between.'

'You don't approve?'

He had finished his pasta and was leaning back in his chair with indolent ease as he sipped his wine.

'It isn't my business to approve or disapprove,' Emma declared evenly, biting into a slice of delicious garlic bread and following it with some *chinotto*.

'You do, however, show some interest in my daughter's welfare.'

She met his gaze with equanimity. 'Are you seeking my opinion, or simply stating an assumption?'

The arrival of the waiter precluded an immediate

answer, and she watched with detached interest as their plates were removed.

'You find it surprising that I might seek your opinion?' Nick drawled, and Emma's stomach gave a slight lurch as she recognised the faint cynicism apparent in his voice.

'If you genuinely want it,' she offered calmly, and watched as his mouth curved into a sardonic smile.

'Now why should you suppose otherwise?' His eyes became faintly hooded, and she could sense their brooding assessment.

It was difficult enough simply sharing his company, without being subjected to an analytical appraisal!

'Because I think you're playing a game,' she responded levelly. 'One in which you intend to amuse yourself at my expense.'

'You're sure of that?' The silkiness evident in his voice set her nerve-ends vibrating in instinctive alarm, despite his apparent indolence.

'Will you deny it?' she countered as she fearlessly met and held his gaze. Her fingers smoothed the napkin on her lap, unconsciously examining the stitched edge before curling into a tight ball.

'The summer holidays are long,' he reflected deliberately. 'During which I arrange to have several weeks free to spend with my daughter. Silvana accords that the process of learning is an ongoing occurrence, no matter how briefly or in what manner the lesson. Hence the adherence to a daily study period prior to my arrival in Rome. Once Silvana departs on her vacation I ensure Annalisa enjoys a relaxing break, and we spend most of the daylight hours together.' One eyebrow rose quizzically, and he queried tolerantly, 'Perhaps we should declare a truce, and begin again?'

'Or you could take me back to the villa.'

'And spoil what promises to be an enjoyable evening?'

'You might take pleasure in baiting me, but I find it distasteful.' She didn't really care if he took umbrage; he had no right to treat her as an interesting specimen and attempt a dissection.

Hidden laughter gleamed from the depths of his eyes, and she became so incensed she was tempted to hit him.

'Silence?'

He was amused, and she seethed inwardly as the waiter appeared with her salad and Nick's veal dish. The atmosphere between them must have been apparent, for the waiter looked momentarily startled as he set both plates down on to the table before he made an unobtrusive but hasty retreat.

The salad looked fresh and inviting, but if she ate one mouthful she would choke! Yet if she pushed it to one side the action would be tantamount to an admission of sorts, and she was darned if she'd give him that satisfaction. Instead she stabbed her fork into the crisp curl of lettuce, fervently wishing that it was Nick Castelli.

Studiously she avoided sparing him so much as a glance, although half-way through her salad she found the temptation unbearable and risked a covert peek beneath long, fringed lashes. To witness, even so briefly, his obvious enjoyment of his meal was sufficient to enrage her further, and at that moment he sensed her regard and levelled a glittering glance that left her in little doubt of his amusement at her antipathy.

Her eyes widened infinitesimally, then warred openly with his own, and it took considerable effort not to pick up her glass and toss the contents in his face.

As if aware of her train of thought, he held her gaze,

deliberately daring her to carry out her silent threat, yet managing to project just what form his retribution would take if she did.

A sudden chill invaded her veins, slipping like ice through her body and cooling her temper. God, what was the matter with her? She had to be mad to even contemplate tangling with him. He seemed curiously intent on unsettling her, arousing anger and a latent animosity she had never even known she possessed.

With a trembling hand she pushed her plate to one side and pretended an interest in their fellow patrons, hearing the quick, fluid chatter, the muted laughter, yet barely registering it as she let her gaze rove sightlessly from table to table.

For one wild moment she considered getting to her feet and walking away, hailing the first taxi that came along and instructing the driver to take her back to the villa. However, such an action would be childish, and she doubted Nick Castelli would permit her such an easy escape. In any case, the evening was still young, and how would she explain to Rosa that she'd chosen to return alone?

It took all her will-power to remain seated in her chair and continue evincing a preoccupation with her surroudings. A lump rose up in her throat, and she swallowed it painfully. It isn't fair, she raged silently. *He's* not being fair. Yet how could she expect a man like Nick Castelli to play by her rules? He was a force unto himself; indomitable and obdurate. If he wanted something, he'd permit no obstacle to stand in his way. Yet what *did* he want? Her companionship for Annalisa in the absence of Silvana? Somehow that answer appeared too simple.

The nerves in her stomach activated themselves and twisted into a palpable knot, pulling cruelly as her emotions began to shred and the pain became a harsh reality that was impossible to ignore.

'Coffee?'

The sound of Nick's voice made her jump, and she missed his narrowed gaze as she kept her head averted.

'No, thank you.' She'd never be able to hold the cup, let alone drink its contents!

The evening dusk had slowly diminished, leaving a velvet sky studded with minuscule far-away stars. Coloured lights suspended at regular intervals provided adequate illumination, and candles flickered inside their ballooned-glass containers on each table.

The long, light, evening hours were difficult to assimilate, together with the continental habit of dining late. The numerous restuarants and bars probably didn't close until three or four each morning!

Emma's thoughts wandered idly to her parents, and she wondered if they were missing her as much as she missed them. The past twelve months had been harmonious, yet at twenty-four she could hardly expect to remain living at home indefinitely. It had been a refuge, a sanctuary where she'd voluntarily given herself into their protective custody, grateful to be shielded from the harsh aftermath of Marc's tragic accident. Perhaps when she returned to Sydney she should think seriously about getting her own apartment.

'Tell me about yourself.'

The soft query startled her, and it took considerable effort to look at him. Only a modicum of good manners was responsible for an attempt at civility, although the words emerged stilted and husky.

'I imagine Rosa and Enzo have already supplied you with a number of pertinent details.'

She saw his eyes darken fractionally, then assume inscrutability.

'Don't be so defensive. It isn't my intention to elicit information you are not prepared to divulge freely.'

'No?' Oh, this was impossible! Here she was, ready to put a cynical connotation on every word he uttered. Drawing a deep breath, she expelled it slowly, then began with contrived politeness, 'I grew up in Sydney, attended private schools, took dancing and music lessons, played tennis in summer and netball in winter. During my mid-teens I developed an interest in co-ordinating fashion accessories with designer garments, and eventually made it my career.'

Nick regarded her silently for several long seconds. 'You have never travelled before?'

'My parents presented me with a return air ticket to London for my twentieth birthday. It was a gift to mark the end of my education, and, they insisted, for being a model daughter.'

A faint gleam of amusement lightened his dark gaze. 'I see. Despite auburn tresses, there were no teenage tantrums, no rebellion against parental authority?'

'We had a few differences of opinion,' Emma allowed. 'But the ground rules were fair, and I saw no reason to thwart them.'

'No boyfriends other than Marc?'

Perhaps she should have been prepared for it, but the query temporarily robbed her of breath, and her lashes fluttered, then lowered, creating a protective shield from his scrutiny.

'When we were young, he was the brother I never had.

We did everything together,' she revealed slowly, hating his imperturbable probing.

'And fell in love.'

Her eyes closed with momentary pain. 'Yes.'

There was a long silence, one that became increasingly difficult to break. Perhaps she should ask a few questions of her own, create an about-face and re-open a few of *his* wounds.

'What of your wife?' She had wanted to hurt as she'd been hurt, but there was no relish in her statement, no demand for his explanation.

'Anna died from a complication associated with Annalisa's birth. She never left the hospital.'

He'd had nine years to recover from the loss, and there was the living bonus of his daughter. Emma had nothing.

'You've never sought to provide Annalisa with a mother?'

He took his time answering, and for a few minutes she thought he wasn't going to; then a wry smile tugged the edge of his mouth.

'One must first find the right woman to marry,' he declared with thinly veiled mockery, and she held his gaze without any difficulty at all.

'Somewhere among the countless number of eligible females beating a path to your door there must be a sincere soul who will love you for yourself and not your worldly possessions.'

'I'm working on it,' Nick drawled, and she effected a faint grimace.

'And enjoying the process of elimination.'

'Are you suggesting I should not?'

His cynicism struck an antagonistic chord, causing her to employ unaccustomed flippancy. 'I hope you've assured whichever young woman I've supplanted this evening that your position as my escort is merely an obligatory duty.'

For a brief second Emma thought she glimpsed anger in the momentary hardening of his eyes, then it was gone, and he leaned well back in his chair to regard her with deceptive indolence.

'I am answerable to no woman.' The words were soft, yet beneath the silk was tensile steel.

Naturally, she agreed silently. There probably wasn't a woman alive who could tame him.

'Perhaps if you've finished your coffee, we could go home,' Emma ventured quietly. 'We've enjoyed a pleasant meal, but it's quite late, and——'

'You need your beauty sleep,' Nick intervened imperturbably.

'Yes.'

'As well as a number of hours in which to fortify yourself against my presence tomorrow,' he added sardonically, and she offered him a brilliant smile.

'Ah, but Annalisa will be with us.'

His eyes gleamed with hidden laughter as he collected the bill and extracted his wallet. 'And her company is infinitely preferable to mine, hmm?'

'I won't answer that.'

He got to his feet and beckoned the waiter, handing over a generous tip—if the man's almost obsequious gratitude was any indication. Then he lightly clasped her elbow and escorted her out to the car.

The drive home was achieved in less than fifteen minutes, and once within the electronically controlled gates he negotiated the driveway and slid the car into the garage situated at the rear of the villa, taking the furthermost bay from a gleaming Alfa Romeo, a Porsche and a functional Fiat.

There was a path leading to a side entrance into the villa through a rose garden, and Emma made her way towards it as Nick secured the garage doors.

Electric lanterns provided a soft, illuminating glow, and the trees lining the boundary seemed to loom incredibly tall in the enshrouding darkness.

A faint prickle of apprehension shivered through her slender frame at the almost eerie stillness, and she wondered if there were spirits of a past civilisation haunting the grounds. Fanciful thinking, she dismissed in self-admonition.

A touch on her arm caused her to jump imperceptibly, and she offered little resistance as Nick fell into step at her side. His nearness was protective, yet she was supremely conscious of him, aware of the faint aroma of his aftershave in the clear evening air, his sheer masculinity and the threat he posed to her equilibrium.

The walk was an incredibly short one, and she released an inaudible sigh as he reached out and unlocked the door.

'Would you care for a nightcap?' he queried as they reached the main hallway. The wall sconces were all alight, but she couldn't detect any sound. 'I doubt Rosa and Enzo will have retired.'

'I'd prefer to go straight to bed,' she declined, unwilling to prolong the evening any further. 'Thank you for taking me to dinner.'

He reached out a hand and trailed his forefinger down the length of her nose. 'Spoken like a well behaved child.'

To stand here like this was madness, and she took a backwards step as he bent his head to bestow a fleeting kiss to her lips; light as the brush of a butterfly's wing, yet it released a flood of warmth that slowly swept through her entire body.

'Ah, there you are! We were about to go upstairs,' Rosa's voice intruded, and Emma looked stricken, her eyes widening with a mixture of guilt and remorse.

For a few timeless seconds she'd been enmeshed in an irresistible pull of the senses, without thought to anything except the moment.

'We have just this minute arrived,' Nick announced smoothly, turning slightly so that his frame provided a partial shield.

Emma took a deep, calming breath and attempted to present a relaxed, smiling façade as she stepped forward. 'It was a lovely meal,' she imparted quietly. 'Nick was right, the food was delicious.' She spared him a quick glance, then she moved forward to touch her lips lightly to the older woman's cheek. 'Goodnight, I'll see you at breakfast in the morning.'

She moved quickly towards the stairs, and had to refrain from running up them as if a hundred demons were chasing at her heels.

It wasn't until she was safely in her room with the door closed behind her that she slumped in a heap on to the bed and buried her face in her hands.

She couldn't be susceptible to Nick Castelli! It was simply a natural feminine reaction to a very attractive man. Even as the thought surfaced, a hollow laugh rose and choked in her throat. There had to be a logical reason for the way she was feeling, yet the only one she recognised had its roots buried in the most base of human needs. Up until now she had thought sex and love went hand in hand; inseparable entities that became entwined in the sexual act itself.

Perhaps, she decided with a sense of desperation, the deep, aching void she experienced could be attributed indirectly to a need for what she had tragically lost.

However, it wasn't Marc's face that clouded her vision, and that seemed to be the ultimate sin.

In a daze she rose to her feet and crossed to the dressing-table. The drawer slid out smoothly, and she extracted a framed photograph. The laughing, boyish face stared back at her, the wide-spaced, bright eyes so alive, his mouth parted in an affectionate, teasing smile.

It was only an image on celluloid. Marc belonged in the past, where perfection ruled, and the present was part of a horrid nightmare.

With careful fingers she placed the frame on the pedestal beside her bed, then she discarded her clothes and slipped between cool percale sheets to lie staring at the ceiling until sedative-induced sleep lulled her into merciful oblivion.

CHAPTER FOUR

DURING the following days, Emma didn't know whether to be pleased or irritated by the number of sightseeing excursions suggested by Annalisa and indulgently fostered by Nick. Certainly she was grateful for their company and factual knowledge as they visited the Sistine Chapel, the Vatican Museum, the Roman Forum and the Colosseum. All were steeped in history, and there was a natural awe in treading such hallowed ground.

There were also scenic trips by car which inevitably included a picnic lunch or a meal eaten at a convenient *trattoria* en route.

Annalisa was a delight, her laughter warm and infectious, regarding everything with such natural enthusiasm it proved to be increasingly difficult for Emma to refuse Nick's continued hospitality. Even Rosa unknowingly aided Annalisa's collusion by developing a mild virus which kept her indoors and thus delayed her own plans to escort Emma to a number of fashionable boutiques.

As for Nick, he was the perfect host and companion; amusing, informal, and Emma found him increasingly impossible to ignore. No matter how she tried to convince herself she was immune to his particular brand of masculinity, each passing day brought an elevated awareness that was positively maddening.

That he *knew*, angered her unbearably, and it was

almost the final straw when, at the conclusion of one breakfast in the second week of her stay, Annalisa excused herself from the table and went in search of a clutch of brochures from which to plot out the day's outing.

'I really can't continue to impose on you like this,' Emma ventured, and incurred his dark, steady glance before he picked up his cup and drained what remained of his coffee.

'My dear Emma, how can your company be an imposition? Besides, think how disappointed my daughter will be if you don't come with us,' he remarked musingly. 'Tomorrow you are to visit some of the city's famed fashion houses with Rosa,' he reminded with unruffled ease. 'Annalisa will have to make do with me, so why not indulge her today?'

His gaze was level, yet his eyes held latent amusement and an element she was unable to define. Damn him, she cursed beneath her breath. He was steadily infiltrating her life, placing her in an increasingly invidious position, where to refuse made her seem exceedingly rude and ungrateful. And he had supposedly innocent assistants in his subterfuge, for if it wasn't Rosa urging her to accept, Annalisa was the mastermind of all matchmakers!

'I would be quite happy to spend the day here, and swim,' she said evenly.

'Is it your intention to be contrary?' His deep, husky laugh was almost her undoing, and she shot him a look of mild antipathy.

'You flatter yourself if you think I sit here quivering at the mere thought of your invitation.'

'*Quivering*, Emma? What an evocative thought,' Nick

mused with a degree of cynicism, then he added softly, 'You sound almost afraid. Are you?'

'Of course not,' she retorted swiftly. Yet deep inside she wasn't so sure. *Damn him!* Who did he think he was, for the love of heaven? Then a hollow laugh rose in her throat. He knew exactly who he was. Not only that, his every action was calculated with implacable precision.

Her eyes slid over his broad shoulders, down to his tapered waist, noting the lean hips, the forceful thrust of muscled thighs beneath the fine material of his trousers. Just by looking at him she could almost feel again the touch of his mouth on hers and, as if possessed of some diabolical form of mental telepathy, he caught her eyes and held them, his gaze steady, missing nothing as they swept her expressive features.

The mere sight of him stirred her senses, reawakening the seeds of desire, and she experienced a feeling of shocked disbelief at the wayward trend of her thoughts. Perhaps it was the aura of power which surrounded him, an elemental magnetism that combined self-assurance and latent sexuality; a dramatic mesh of male charisma that was infinitely dangerous.

'Shall we endeavour to get away about eight-thirty?'

His voice was a mocking drawl, and she was darned if she'd meekly comply. Unbidden, the germ of an idea took root in her mind, and she directed him a look that appeared completely without guile.

'Very well, if you insist.' Her eyes assumed a deep tawny hue. 'Will you mind if I browse among some of the boutiques and shop for clothes? A devilish imp prompted her to offer him a singularly sweet smile. 'You'll probably be bored to death.'

'Annalisa, however, will be in her element,' he responded lazily, and without a further word she rose to her feet and made her way upstairs to change into suitable attire, hollowly aware that she had been defeated.

Three hours later his arms held a variety of multi-coloured packages and carrier-bags, and the sight of such an obviously masculine man thus encumbered brought forth a devilish smile.

'Are you suffering?'

'Wasn't it your intention that I should?'

That he was aware of her perversity merely made her determined to prolong the shopping expedition. 'I haven't finished yet,' she declared blithely as she caught sight of a shop displaying exquisite lingerie. 'Perhaps you'd prefer to wait outside. I won't be long.'

One eyebrow rose with quizzical mockery. 'Why should you imagine I will be embarrassed? The female form adorned in such wispy fripperies holds no surprises for me.' His eyes gleamed with merciless humour. 'You may even appreciate my opinion.'

Before she had the opportunity to demur he moved into the shop, utilised deliberate charm with the young assistant, then proceeded to indicate a selection of garments which he considered flattering—for Emma, as well as Annalisa.

It left her feeling helplessly angry, although she had no intention of letting him guess he'd got beneath her skin.

'Shall we deposit these in the car, then find somewhere to have lunch?' Nick suggested blandly when they emerged out on to the pavement.

'Yes, please, *Papa*. I am *hungry*,' Annalisa agreed with alacrity.

Food. Now that she gave it some thought, she was ravenous. Besides, the heat was beginning to have an enervating effect, and the thought of walking the city's streets no longer held any appeal, especially as everything would soon close for the afternoon.

'Thank you.' She even managed a faint smile.

Nick chose a charming *ristorante* and ordered wine while Emma perused the menu, selecting after very little deliberation a portion of *lasagne* which, when it duly arrived, proved to be utterly delicious.

'I adore the dress you bought,' Annalisa enthused as she forked pasta into her mouth. 'I can't wait until I am old enough to wear something like that.'

'A few years yet, *piccina*,' Nick commented indulgently, and Emma offered the young girl a sincere smile.

'You'll knock all the boys for six,' she assured her gently, adding with a touch of humour and a quick glance towards the man at her side, 'and doubtless give your father a few extra grey hairs in the process.'

'Do you think so?' Annalisa asked, clearly intrigued.

'About the grey hairs? Assuredly,' concluded her father wryly.

'I have just had a wonderful idea. Why don't you take Emma out to dinner tonight?' Her eyes sparkled with youthful enthusiasm and the sureness of one who is convinced of success. 'Emma could wear her new dress.'

'Why not, indeed?' Nick concurred smoothly, and Emma met his gaze, her eyes cool and infinitely clear.

'Perhaps we should first check with Rosa? She may have made plans which include us.'

Rosa hadn't, and expressed delight that her godson intended escorting Emma to dinner—so much so that, between Rosa and Annalisa, Emma didn't stand a chance.

The calf-length dress in deep turquoise silk-textured fabric possessed a pin-pleated skirt which floated softly with every movement she made, while its camisole-styled bodice with twin shoestring straps over each shoulder lent emphasis to her slim curves and accentuated the delicate glow of her skin. Slim-heeled gold evening sandals, a gold chain at her throat and matching bracelet at her wrist added understated elegance, and to complete the outfit she added a silk beaded evening jacket in matching turquoise. The whole effect was stunning, and she stood back, pleased with her mirrored image.

Nick was waiting in the lounge, a crystal tumbler in one hand, looking the epitome of male sophistication in a dark superbly tailored evening suit, pale blue shirt and a black bow-tie. He exuded more than his fair share of raw virility, and Emma felt her pulse-beat quicken and begin an erratic, hammering tattoo.

'This is becoming something of a habit,' she declared almost ten minutes later as Nick eased the Ferrari through the impressive gates guarding entrance to the villa.

'Hardly that. This is only the second occasion we have dined out in the evening. Most nights have been spent at the villa in the company of Rosa, Enzo and Annalisa, have they not?' he queried smoothly.

It was true, for she had enjoyed the family atmosphere generated by Rosa and Enzo, the games of cards and the lengthy discussion over a leisurely meal.

'Where are we dining?' she queried lightly.

'I've reserved a table at a restaurant on the *Piazza Navona*,' Nick informed, concentrating on urging the car through the flow of traffic. 'Parking within walking distance will be almost impossible, and the attempt merely time consuming. Hence the need for a taxi for a minimum few kilometres.'

The establishment he'd chosen was well patronised, its décor steeped in traditional elegance, and the service they were accorded held the impressive deference normally reserved for the rich and famous.

'You come here often.' It was an observation, never a query, and his answering smile held a touch of cynicism.

'Whenever I am in Rome, yes,' he conceded, and she felt a tingle of pink colour her cheeks that he might have guessed her thoughts. 'The chef treats the preparation of food with practised artistry, hence the result is always a gastromic delight.'

'You are an obvious connoisseur,' she commented drily, and incurred his dark, slanting glance.

'Food, specifically, of course,' he drawled with hateful mockery.

'Naturally. Although I don't doubt such superiority extends to every sphere,' she offered sweetly, and caught the gleam of silent laughter in the depths of his eyes.

'Especially of women. Isn't that what you meant to imply?'

She met his gaze unflinchingly. 'Perhaps I find it difficult to believe you would accord entertaining the widow of a distant relative anything but a boring duty.'

Now he did laugh, a mocking, husky chuckle that hit an exposed nerve and made her feel vaguely uncertain.

'Boring, Emma? How could an enchanting auburn-haired young woman whose golden cat's eyes hide a multitude of emotions be regarded as anything other than intriguing?' An eyebrow lifted in quizzical query, and she was unable to suppress the tingle of electricity that filtered through her veins.

'Don't regard me as a challenge, Nick.' For some reason she felt like a butterfly caught in a trap, and unsure whether fate would be kind or cruel. Her eyes swept to meet his, widening measurably at his unwavering regard.

'Relax,' he bade silkily. 'I have no intention of harming so much as a hair on your beautiful head.'

If only she could believe him! He possessed an elemental charisma to which most women would be attracted, as a moth to flame, perhaps uncaring that such captivating appeal could lead to their own destruction.

'Have some wine,' he coaxed quietly, and she obediently lifted the fluted goblet to her lips and savoured its contents, glad of the slow warmth that crept soothingly through her body.

'Shall we order?' Nick inclined smoothly. 'I suggest *fettucini al funghi* as a starter, followed by breasts of chicken in a delicate honey and almond sauce. I prefer salad, but there is a choice of hot vegetables available.'

It was at least an escape to pretend an interest in the menu, and despite a fondness for mushroom sauce with pasta she elected to settle for spaghetti *marinara* with a salad to follow.

If he perceived her selection as a small act of defiance he made no comment, and merely sipped his wine, while

Emma let her gaze skim round the room with seeming fascination.

'Annalisa has persuaded me to coach her at tennis tomorrow while you are out with Rosa, followed by a swim in the pool.'

His lazy smile was warm and reached his eyes, and she said with total sincerity, 'Annalisa is a delightful child.'

'Yes. We are very close.'

The pasta was delicious, and she forked it into her mouth with practised ease. She was no stranger to Italian-style food, for Marc's mother was an excellent cook and Emma had shared Sunday dinner with Marc and his parents for almost as long as she could remember.

'*Caro!* How wonderful to see you.'

Emma turned slightly and caught sight of a stunning brunette who looked as if she'd just stepped out from between the pages of *Vogue*. Tall and superbly slender, her dress was a Dior original. Diamonds studded each earlobe, a matching choker graced her neck, and her classical features portrayed a flawless skin exquisitely adorned with skilfully applied make-up. Perfume, easily identifiable as Dior's *Poison*, exuded from her body in a soft, wafting cloud.

It was obvious she exulted in being the focus of attention. Also apparent was her adoration of Nick, for her eyes swept over him with thinly veiled hunger before swinging back to the man at her side.

Emma let her gaze drift as Nick stood to his feet and performed introductions with sophisticated ease.

'Danielle, my cousin Vincenzo. Emma Martinero.'

Danielle Fabrese. Emma wondered why visual recognition of the internationally famous model hadn't been synonymous, then it registered. The hairstyle. Previously shoulder-length and worn in a contrived windblown look, the model's tresses were now much shorter and cut to give her delicately boned face an elfin appearance.

'You have no objection if we join you?' The query was delivered with deliberate coquetry and gave Nick little opportunity to refuse as Danielle instructed a hovering and obviously enamoured waiter to increase the seating arrangements by two.

'Vince, order more wine, *piacere*,' the model implored with a faint, pouting smile. 'I am thirsty.'

'Perrier?' His teeth gleamed white. 'I refuse to be the subject of your wrath if a glass or two of wine tips the scales against you tomorrow.'

There was a family resemblance between the two men, slight but evident none the less, Emma perceived. However, Vince was younger by a few years, and lacked four or five inches of his cousin's height.

There was something vaguely amusing in being an innocent observer, Emma conceded as the meal progressed. Nick portrayed smooth-spoken urbanity without any effort at all, while appearing seemingly detached from the effect of Danielle's scintillating charm. He gave the appearance of being fascinated, but the keenest eye could detect that the attraction was merely superficial, and Emma couldn't help but wonder why. The model had it all; beauty, personality, fame. She could have any man she wanted with the merest flick of her exquisitely curled eyelashes. Except, maybe, Nick Castelli. Perhaps she *had* had him, Emma decided, for it didn't take much perception to read the sexual tension evident in the other woman's manner.

Whatever the reason, it seemed one-sided, and Emma felt a pang of pity. To be rejected by a man must be hell, especially someone like Nick Castelli. Perhaps that was why Danielle monopolised the conversation with witty anecdotes, and deliberately indulged in according Vince a number of adoring glances in the hope that Nick might be swayed towards jealousy.

A faint grimace flitted momentarily across Emma's features. Somehow she couldn't imagine Nick being the jealous type. He possessed sufficient nous to enable him to hold any woman he chose to pursue, and he was enough of a chauvinist to insist on being the hunter rather than the hunted.

'Martinero. The name is Italian,' Danielle declared with a careless gesture of her exquisitely manicured hand. 'But you are not, I think?'

Emma unconsciously stiffened, aware of a certain malevolence evident in the model's polite query. She caught the swift, spearing glance the brunette accorded to the ring adorning her left hand and was aware of the speculative interest it aroused.

'My husband was Australian-born of Italian parents,' Emma explained quietly.

'*Was?*' Danielle repeated with delicate emphasis.

'Yes.' She met the other girl's glittery gaze with remarkable steadiness, considering the discordant state of her nerves. 'Marc was killed in a car accident last year.'

There was an imperceptible silence, followed by an audible breathy sigh. 'Ah, I see. How sad for you.'

She didn't look in the least sad, Emma decided disparagingly.

'How kind of Nick to take pity on you.' The smile was fixed, curving her luscious mouth into a mere facsimile. 'I presume you are holidaying in Italy?'

'Emma is Rosa's and Enzo's granddaughter-in-law,' Nick revealed indolently, and Danielle's eyes hardened with instant comprehension.

'Then you are both staying at the villa.'

The air crackled with latent animosity, and Emma's eyes widened slightly as Nick drawled, 'Yes. You are aware Annalisa and I spend each summer vacation with Rosa and Enzo.'

'So—convenient, Emma, for you to have timed your visit to coincide with that of Nick's,' Danielle shifted her attention with a swift flick of her immaculately mascara-brushed lashes. 'I can vouch he is an attentive and amusing companion.' For a brief second the lashes swept upward and her eyes fixed Emma with a venomous glare, then it was masked as she centred her attention on her companion. 'Vince, we must call on Nick while he is at the Martinero villa. You are related, after all. How long are you staying, Emma?'

'Three weeks altogether.' It was on the tip of her tongue to explain she had been barely aware of Nick Castelli's existence until last week, and that if she had known Rosa and Enzo were entertaining guests, she would never have come to Italy.

'Would you care to dance with me, Emma?'

She turned slightly and glimpsed Nick's faintly hooded gaze. The slightly cynical edge to his tone brought a defiant sparkle to her eyes, and she was sorely tempted to refuse.

If they had been alone, she would have had no

hesitation, and his lips twisted fractionally in recognition of her indecision. Damn him, he knew she had little choice but to agree. To do otherwise would only play into Danielle's hands, and Emma was darned if she'd give the model that satisfaction.

The restaurant wasn't large, and the floorspace allocated for dancing could only be described as inadequate.

Perhaps she should have been prepared for the inevitability of physical contact, the strangeness of being in another man's arms. Dancing hadn't been one of Marc's favoured pursuits, and she felt awkward, ill at ease, and all too aware that being held by Nick Castelli was a highly evocative experience, despite his conventional hold. Some mystical, illusory chemistry had to be responsible for the tingling warmth that sprang to life and began pulsing through her veins.

'Relax,' he bade quietly, but it was easier said than done, and when the music quickened in tempo she moved backwards, out of his grasp, her features pale.

'I think I'd like to go——' She almost said 'home', except home was several thousand kilometres distant, on the other side of the world. 'To the villa. If you don't mind.' She added the last few words as an afterthought, and missed his narrowed gaze.

'Soon. An early escape will be seen to be precisely that, and I am damned if I will allow Danielle to win a slight advantage and use it against you.'

'Should I take that as a compliment?'

'You are fathoms out of your depth, *cara*,' he drawled. 'Why not appear to be enjoying each other's company?'

'And dance?' Her nerves seemed to be shredding into a

thousand threads, and her eyes mirrored an anguish that went right down to the depths of her soul.

'Would it be such a hardship?'

She caught his smile as he gently pulled her back into his arms. His hold was possessive, almost intimate, and she attempted to move back without success.

'Tell me,' she ventured evenly, lifting her head to look at him, then she immediately wished she hadn't for his face was far too close. Another inch, and her lips would brush his. 'Is this necessary?'

A faint gleam of amusement entered his eyes, and she could cheerfully have hit him. 'I won't be used,' she declared tightly.

She felt him stiffen, then he murmured with deceptive calm, 'You imagine I am deliberately attempting to establish you as my latest—conquest, shall we say?'

She had the oddest feeling he'd like to shake her until she begged for mercy, and a tiny shiver shook her slim frame.

'Thus making it painfully clear to Danielle that my interest lies elsewhere, and she should give up the foolish notion of pursuing me,' he inclined with dangerous softness. 'Is that what you think?'

'The possibility did occur.'

His teeth gleamed white in the subdued lighting, and she suppressed the urge to slap the wry amusement from his face.

'Danielle has a burning ambition to lure me into her manipulative net, and attempting to ensnare me has become something of an unenviable obsession.' His voice assumed mocking cynicism. 'The ironic part of it all is that if she succeeded the excitement would end, and I would be discarded without further thought.'

'I'm filled with compassion,' Emma remarked drily, and a soft, husky laugh emerged from his throat.

'Really?' he derided quietly.

She threw him a dark glance as she corrected sweetly, 'For Danielle. All that time wasted on a man who couldn't care less.'

'You make me sound like an inveterate rake.'

'And you're not?'

'There is one woman for whom I care very much.'

Her heart gave an imperceptible jolt, then steadied and resumed its normal beat. 'If she has an ounce of sense,' she declared lightly, 'she'll keep you dangling on a string to the very end.'

One eyebrow quirked in silent amusement, and Emma reiterated without humour, 'I don't imagine you've reached your thirties without being aware of the devastating effect you have on the female sex.'

'You being the exception, hmm?'

'I'm not interested in forming a liaison with any man.'

'Would you deny yourself another man's love— children?' His breath stirred her hair and she gave a sudden start as his lips brushed against her temple.

He sounded serious—too serious, and the breath caught in her throat as she endeavoured to control the way her pulse leapt out of control and began to thud visibly in the hollow at the base of her neck. He was treading dangerous ground, and she lifted her head and met his dark gaze. Not only met it, but she managed to hold it long enough to see the faint narrowing evident.

'Shall we go back and join Danielle and Vince?'

If looks could kill, she would be dead, Emma decided

when they reached the table, for Danielle's glittery gaze was full of thin veiled animosity.

'Really, Nick,' the model remonstrated in a soft, purring voice. 'You cannot be permitted to monopolise Signora Martinero in such a manner.'

'Emma is a valued guest,' Nick drawled silkily, and Emma took the utmost pleasure in turning slightly towards him as she offered a deliberately sweet smile.

'As a long-standing friend, Danielle has every right to feel neglected.'

It was impossible to read anything from his expression, apart from an initial flaring of something indefinable in the depths of his eyes, and she watched in mesmerised fascination as he reached out and caught hold of her hand.

'If you will excuse us?' He let his gaze encompass Danielle and Vince, and without waiting for their response he collected Emma's wrap.

For a moment she was tempted to resist, just for the sheer hell of it, then common sense overrode obstinacy as she made her farewell while Nick settled the bill.

'There is no need for you to take the role of my companion so seriously,' she declared as they reached the pavement. 'I won't be held responsible for inhibiting your social life.'

'Hasn't it occurred to you that I might prefer your company?'

She shot him a searching glance. 'Why?'

'Why not?' Nick parried blandly, taking hold of her arm as they began strolling along the *piazza* in search of a taxi.

'We rarely agree on anything.'

'Perhaps I see you as a refreshing change from most women of my acquaintance.'

'Who elect to hang on to your every word,' Emma opined drily, and heard his faint chuckle.

'Their motive is transparent at best.'

She nodded in mute agreement. 'Ah, yes! You must be quite a catch.'

'Don't be facetious,' he chided musingly. 'It doesn't suit you.'

'Why deny the truth?' Some demoniacal imp was urging her on, when every sane cell in her body cautioned she should desist. 'You're the embodiment of every quality attributed to the Italian male.' She subjected his lengthy frame to a deliberate, assessing appraisal. 'Tall, attractive. Attentive, pleasant, and eminently successful.' She pretended contemplation. 'There's a touch of arrogance apparent and a trend towards chauvinism, but aside from that I guess there's not much to detract from the image.'

'It's as well I don't beat young women or children,' Nick drawled with hateful cynicism, and she affected a stunning smile.

'Why, Nick,' she chastised softly, 'I could never attribute you with an act of violence.'

'Whereas you, sweet Emma, seem hellbent on treading a path towards provoking it.'

'Is that a threat?'

'The choice of interpretation is entirely yours.'

What on earth was the matter with her? It was as if she'd taken a stick and was intent on prodding a sleeping tiger. To what end? His retribution would be swift and deadly, and inevitably cause her pain of a kind she'd be wise to avoid.

She lapsed into silence, and was grateful when he successfully hailed a passing taxi. Maintaining silence, she stared beyond the windscreen and emerged when they reached the parked Ferrari.

Within minutes she slid into the passenger seat and watched with idle fascination as he fired the engine prior to sending the sleek vehicle into the flow of late-evening traffic.

His movements were smooth and sure, and Emma felt the soft hammering of her pulse in sheer reaction to his close proximity. He possessed a potent animalistic sense of power that succeeded in making her feel unaccountably cross and at odds with herself—worse, in the knowledge that some dark, swirling emotion was beginning to take root that had no basis in her existence. At least, not one of which she wanted any part. Impossible to define precisely what it was that bothered her. An expression, the intensity of his gaze; the sureness with which he was invading her life—even contriving to fashion it to his own advantage.

His daughter was a charming child, so earnest and caring, and whose affection for a remote Australian relative-by-marriage was daily becoming increasingly more obvious. In a way it wasn't fair to kindle such fondness, yet to discourage it was beyond Emma's capability.

'You're very quiet.'

She turned slowly to look at him in the darkness of the car's interior, and glimpsed the strong angles and planes of his profile in the reflection of light from a passing car.

'I thought you'd prefer to give illuminating conversation a miss and concentrate on driving.'

'How considerate,' he mocked softly. 'I was convinced you had chosen to disregard me.'

'Not at all,' she disclaimed, and missed the faint gleam in his eyes as she returned her attention to the passing night-time scenery.

Her eyelids began to feel heavy, and she wasn't aware she had slipped into a fitful doze until she felt a hand on her shoulder.

'Emma.'

She opened her eyes, and nothing looked familiar. 'Where are we?'

'The Villa d'Este,' Nick informed. 'A spectacular vista at night with the fountains lit—definitely a sight worth seeing.' He leaned across and unlatched her door. 'Come, we will walk through the gardens.'

His arm brushed the curve of her breast, and she was powerless to still the frisson of fear that began somewhere deep inside and intensified at his accidental touch.

Without a word she slipped out from the car and stood waiting as he crossed to her side.

'Five hundred fountains,' Nick revealed quietly. 'Aren't they magnificent?'

It was a magical fairyland with cascading water creating a multitude of pulsating dance sequences that varied and delighted with every movement.

'They're beautiful,' Emma breathed, spellbound. Her eyes were alive, her lips parted in receptive pleasure.

'Yes.'

Something in the tone of his voice alerted her attention, and she turned towards him in seeming slow motion as his hands settled on her shoulders.

'Please—don't,' she whispered as he impelled her forward, and at once the butterflies in her stomach began an erratic tattoo, making her frighteningly aware of the electric awareness between them.

Emma felt herself begin to tremble, and when she attempted to extricate herself from the enforced intimacy of his arms he lowered his head and touched his lips briefly against her temple.

'Nick——' She didn't care if she beseeched him, she was even prepared to beg—anything, for if he kissed her, nothing would ever be the same again.

The appeal was useless, and a further protest became lost as his mouth slid down to cover hers in a kiss that was tantalising, tender, yet with a hint of controlled passion and fleetingly brief.

To her utter chagrin it left her feeling vaguely bereft and wanting more. Then reaction set in, and with it came anger. 'How dare you!'

Nick was silent for several seconds, then he slowly shook his head. 'Oh, I dare, Emma,' he mocked gently.

'Let me go,' she whispered furiously.

'Really, *cara*,' he reproved in a hateful drawl, 'I fail to comprehend a reason for such anger.'

'Next you'll tell me your intentions are strictly honourable, I suppose?' She was so consumed with antipathy that her whole body was beginning to shake with it.

'Are you so sure they are not?'

Her eyes widened, dilating with confusion and, conscious of the painful thudding of her heart, she forced herself to breathe slowly in an effort to gain some measure of control.

'If this is a game,' she indicated unsteadily, 'I don't want to play.'

'Afraid I might win?'

'After which I go my way, you go yours, and thanks for the memory?' she spat out with unaccustomed bitterness. The thought of attempting further conversation with him tonight was almost more than she could bear, and she desperately needed to get away from him.

'Please take me back to the villa.'

'So you can be alone, to cry?' His eyes were dark, their expression unfathomable. 'All the tears in the world won't bring Marc back.'

The stark cruelty of his words brought a shocked gasp from her lips. 'How dare you speak to me like that?' she whispered, her face ashen.

'Someone should.'

Resentment began to rise to the surface at his apparent callousness, and she momentarily closed her eyes in an attempt to regain her composure.

'And you've elected yourself, I suppose?'

He regarded her silently for what seemed an age, then the edge of his mouth twisted into a sardonic smile. 'I consider I have a vested interest.'

Helpless anger flared, and her eyes assumed a golden brilliance as she swept his broad frame with a wrathful, encompassing glare. 'Oh? What comes next?' She tipped her head back to meet his impenetrable scrutiny. 'Some misguided homily about wanting to *help* me?'

He looked at her in silence and, defeated, she let her lashes slowly flicker down to blot out his forceful image.

Then her eyes flew wide as his hands cupped her face,

and surprise kept her transfixed as his head lowered until
his mouth was on hers, brushing the outline of her lips in
a slow, evocative movement that made her gasp.

She stood still, shocked into immobility as his kiss
became warm and probing, his touch disruptively
sensual as he brought her close against him, holding her
fast without any effort at all. Then, with unhurried ease,
he sought the soft, inner sweetness of her mouth.

A silent moan rose in her throat, then died, as he
savoured the inner recesses with an infinite degree of
sensuality, and when she attempted to close her teeth he
caught hold of her lower lip and gently pulled it between
his own.

Outraged indignation rose to the fore, and without
thought she relaxed her jaw, only to groan impotently at
her own folly as his mouth moved on hers, effecting a
deliberately flagrant exploration; teasing, tantalising in
a manner that promised much but delivered little, pacing
with unlimited patience in an attempt to evoke her initial
response.

She wouldn't kiss him back, she *wouldn't*! Yet slowly
her resolve began to dissipate, and just as she thought she
could stand it no longer he lifted his head and she stood
immobile, her face devoid of colour and her eyes wide,
deep pools mirroring pain and a degree of self-
humiliation.

Without a word he lifted a hand and trailed his fingers
gently down her cheek, then moved to trace the curve of
her lower lip. 'Don't look like that,' he berated softly.

Emma wasn't able to utter a sound, and tears welled in
her eyes, shimmering, then spilled over to run slowly

down in twin rivulets to rest against the corners of her mouth.

'You sweet fool,' Nick cursed huskily, his eyes dark and unfathomable as he witnessed her desolation.

She felt infinitely fragile, vulnerable, and possessed of a strange complexity of sensibilities that had no part of her past.

'I'd like you to take me home.' Was that her voice? It sounded so bleak and forlorn.

Without a word he took hold of her arm and led the way back to the car.

They seemed to reach the villa in a very short time, and immediately the car slid to a halt inside the garage she slipped out and stood waiting while he locked up.

Indoors, she preceded him to the base of the curving staircase. Before she could ascend he reached out and caught hold of her arm and pulled her close.

She could feel his intent scrutiny, and was overcome with an inexplicable apprehension. It was almost as if he was deliberately adopting an urbane façade in an attempt to put her at ease, and she felt decidedly wary. One false word or move and she'd be catapulted into an explosive situation.

'Don't——'

Her remonstrance was lost as his mouth closed over hers in a brief, passionate kiss, then she was free.

'Goodnight, *cara*.'

Without a backward glance he turned and moved up the stairs, and Emma watched his broad back disappear with a composite of shock and indignation. How dared he kiss her like that! Dear lord, she couldn't remember being so consumed with anger.

Something deep within seemed to be urging her towards a confrontation, tempting her to taunt in a manner that was the antithesis of her nature. She'd never lost her temper with Marc, nor felt the need to offer a differing opinion, let alone argue. Yet with Nick Castelli she experienced a whole gamut of emotions, the least desirable of all being a growing awareness of her own sensuality. Perhaps that was why she disliked him so much, she reflected, as she made her way to the sanctuary of her room.

CHAPTER FIVE

Rosa proved to be an amusing companion, informative and seemingly untiring as she strolled with Emma through the city's streets, frequenting several boutiques where a number of garments took their eye and a selected few were purchased.

Giorgio Armani had created a delightful range, and Emma gazed enviously at a silk-beaded gown by Karl Lagerfeld, seriously tempted, although after much thought she reluctantly decided against it. From a fashion viewpoint, Lagerfeld's theme was body-hugging and only for the very slender figure.

'What it is to be young,' Rosa murmured with a warm smile as they viewed a further selection. 'So many of the designs appear so extreme.'

'I'd hate to be a buyer,' Emma responded quietly. 'Working a season ahead, gauging consumer appeal and taking responsibility for such a huge financial outlay.' A faint smile curved her generous mouth. 'After all, there's no fashion if a projected line doesn't catch on, and viewing various designer collections is accorded such glamour it would be difficult not to be swayed at the time.'

'You enjoy your job, don't you?'

'Yes,' Emma accorded simply. 'Co-ordinating accessories with a garment can be tremendously inspiring. I like to study the client—her mannerisms, her choice of make-up and hairstyle, and most important of all, the image she wants to project. I assemble the basics, shoes, belts, even tights. Then I move on to jewellery, preferring to view her own before suggesting a new purchase.' A faint, mischievous smile lightened her features. 'Although few clients object to spending their husband's money!'

'Especially if the clientele are wealthy,' Rosa declared, and Emma's smile widened, then assumed a certain wryness.

'Yes. Some will simply buy a *name* label just for the sake of being able to claim ownership, regardless of whether or not it suits them.'

'Cynical, but all too accurate,' Rosa agreed. 'One sees the result on frequent occasions, and shudders at their appalling lack of taste.'

They were carrying a number of assorted packages in various carrier-bags which were beginning to prove cumbersome.

'Shall we leave?' Rosa suggested as they completed yet another purchase from a particularly exclusive boutique. 'By the time Carlo attempts to brave the traffic, it will be at least eight before we reach the villa.'

'I think so. We've done very well.'

Rosa turned to the manageress and requested the use of her telephone to summon Carlo with the car, and they waited patiently until the large silver sedan slid in to the kerb, then they seated themselves in the cool, air-conditioned interior while the chauffeur deftly stowed their purchases into the capacious boot.

'What a lovely day it's been,' the older woman enthused with genuine warmth as the car purred its way out of the city. 'I adore your new ensemble. You must wear it to the theatre tonight.' She placed a hand over one of Emma's and patted it gently. 'So very fortunate a colleague of Enzo's gave us two spare tickets, although the poor man was not to know Enzo and I had already seen the play.'

'Very fortunate,' Emma concurred, almost resigned at having been manoeuvred into an evening at the theatre with Nick. Circumstances seemed to contrive against her where he was concerned, and she entertained no doubts that he utilised every available one to his own advantage.

The tranquility of the villa after the city's bustling streets acted like a soothing balm, and a shower did wonders to restore Emma's energy.

Electing to wear the new pale lemon-yellow skirt and matching top Emma added a silver belt to her waist and fastened a wide silver bracelet over her wrist. Make-up came next, and she applied eyeshadow and mascara with skilful ease, then added blusher and coloured her lips with a soft, clear pink.

Emerging downstairs she entered the lounge to find Nick deep in conversation with Enzo.

Impeccable tailoring merely accentuated his tautly muscled frame, and she noted the proud angle of his head, the strength apparent in the powerful set of his shoulders.

Her pulse leapt, then quickened as a thousand tiny nerve-endings surged into pulsating life, and she fought off the treacherous ache that began somewhere in the region of her stomach. It was maddening the way her body was reacting, she decided dispassionately as she moved further into the room.

At that moment he turned, and she was held an

unwilling prisoner by the sudden brilliance in his eyes, the latent passion, and she felt immeasurably afraid.

'Emma, my dear,' Enzo greeted her effusively. 'Do have a drink. What can I get you?

'A mineral water, please,' she requested, offering him a gentle smile before glancing towards Nick, whose dark eyes pinned hers, their gleaming depths alive with cynical amusement.

'The need for a clear head, Emma?'

She directed him a quick glance that was remarkably steady. 'Not at all.'

'Here you are,' Enzo proferred a slim crystal goblet filled with clear, sparkling liquid. '*Salute*,' he bade genially, watching as she sipped the refreshing mineral water. 'I gather you enjoyed your day exploring the various fashion houses with Rosa?'

'Yes,' Emma declared sincerely. 'The clothes are fabulous.'

'And what of tonight, Emma?' Nick parried smoothly. 'Are you looking forward to my company with equal pleasure?'

'But of course,' she responded evenly. 'I'm quite sure you can be guaranteed to entertain me with gentlemanly decorum.' Her sweet smile looked utterly genuine, and from the corner of her eyes she glimpsed Enzo's benevolent observance of their exchange.

'Emma, Nick—please excuse the delay in joining you,' Rosa offered apologetically as she moved towards them. 'A telephone call. Not important, but one which proved difficult to terminate. *Caro*,' she murmured gratefully as Enzo placed a glass of wine in her hand. 'Where is Annalisa?'

'Asleep,' Nick revealed with a slow smile. 'We played several games of tennis, followed by more than an hour in the pool. Then we took a picnic lunch and drove until my daughter discovered a grassy slope deemed suitably picturesque on which to spread a blanket and eat our simple fare.' His shoulders lifted in a negligible shrug as he slanted them each a musing glance. 'The combination of sunshine, exercise and food, without the benefit of an afternoon siesta, took their toll, I'm afraid.'

'Poor *piccina*,' Rosa sympathised warmly.

'If you will excuse us, we will leave, Nick intimated, placing his empty tumbler down on to a nearby table.

'Enjoy yourselves,' said Rosa with a gentle smile. 'We will look forward to seeing you both at breakfast.'

Emma permitted Nick to lead her out to where the Ferrari was parked, and she slid into the passenger seat and fastened the safety-belt with quick sure movements, aware of a sense of misgiving at spending several hours in his company.

A dozen times in as many minutes she summoned the words to begin some meaningless conversational gambit, then she discarded them as being completely inane.

'Don't look so serious. The play has received good reviews. I'm sure you'll enjoy it.'

'Good heavens,' Emma protested mildly, 'I'm not difficult to please.'

Nick's glance was swift and infinitely mocking. 'Indeed?'

A faint tinge of colour rose to her cheeks at his implication, and the look she flung him would have felled a lesser man. 'If I remain in your presence for much longer I'm liable to *hit* you!'

'You rise to the bait so beautifully,' Nick declared. 'Like a miniature virago.'

'Be careful I don't decide to erupt!' She was so angry the emotion seemed to consume her, and its magnitude was quite frightening.

'I am sure I can handle such an event—and its aftermath,' Nick declared silkily, leaving her in little doubt as to how he would deal with it.

She shivered as icy fingers scudded stealthily down her spine, for the mere thought of being subdued by him shook her composure and tore it to shreds. Faced with imagining Nick in the role of lover made her sick with apprehension. He was no insecure beginner, unsure and unaware how to please.

'Do you derive satisfaction from taunting me?' Her voice sounded alien to her ears, and almost afraid.

He shot her a quick, discerning glance, then stifled a savage oath. 'What do you think I intend, for the love of God?'

'I don't know—I don't care,' Emma flung incautiously as she drew a shaky breath. 'I'm tired of being manipulated—by *everyone*.'

'Me, especially.'

'Yes, damn you!' Stupid, angry tears welled up and teetered precariously, ready to spill.

'I could shake you, do you know that?' Nick threatened with dangerous softness, and she retaliated swiftly, 'Why don't you? You've done everything else.'

There was a mesmeric silence, intensifying until she became conscious of every breath she took.

'On the contrary, I haven't put a hand out of place.'

'I wouldn't let you!'

'My dear Emma,' he drawled silkily. 'Do you really think you could stop me?'

'I'd have a damn good try!'

His expression lightened fractionally, and a glint of cynical amusement lit his darkened gaze. 'Yes, I do believe you would.'

'And don't call me your *dear* Emma,' she snapped furiously.

'Why, *cara?*' The cynicism became vaguely mocking. 'Does it bother you so much?'

'I'll never be your—*anything*,' she assured emotionally.

'We have arrived,' Nick drawled, and Emma realised with a start of surprise that the car was stationary.

'Shall we aim for disarmed neutrality?'

'I doubt that's possible,' she muttered, unable to believe they could spend an hour without being at cross-purposes—let alone several.

Nick slid out from behind the wheel, locked his door, then he crossed round to her side of the car. Taking her elbow, he led the way towards a sprawling *piazza*.

'Nevertheless, we shall try, hmm?'

They walked several blocks in companionable silence, and gradually Emma began to relax, dismissing most of her former anxiety as rational logic rose to the surface. Maybe she was over-reacting, having become too aware of her own vulnerability.

Having gained the theatre foyer they were led to a small table with an excellent view of the stage, and in a moment of recklessness Emma ordered a Galliano cocktail, then when it came she sipped it and was dismayed at its potency.

'Have you always lived with your parents?'

She almost choked at the unexpectedness of his query, and took several seconds to form her reply. 'Yes. Apart from the week I was married to Marc.'

Nick's eyes narrowed thoughtfully, and his voice was deceptively bland as he bade, 'Tell me about him.'

Emma had the greatest difficulty in swallowing the lump in her throat, and her voice held a trace of bitterness. 'I'm sure Rosa has told you everything you want to know.'

'Not the things I want to hear.'

She forced her eyes to remain steady beneath his intent gaze, hating him for placing her in such an invidious position. What could she say? Why *should* she say anything?

Nick was silent for what seemed an age, then he ventured with soft deliberation. 'You have an untouched quality—almost as if the heights and depths of passionate ecstasy still remain an elusive mystery.'

A cold anger began to burn inside her, and she threw him a baleful glare. 'Are you implying that I didn't love Marc?'

His hard, intent stare played havoc with her equilibrium. 'Love takes many forms.'

'And you're an expert, of course.' Her scepticism was clearly evident, and his mouth moved to form a sardonic smile.

'My experience has to be considerably more vast than yours.'

'I wouldn't doubt it!' The look she flung him conveyed disparagement, and his answering chuckle came out low and husky, and full of indolent humour.

'Has anyone told you how beautiful you are when you're angry?'

'I've never been sufficiently incensed for anyone to tell me,' she hissed furiously.

'The play is about to begin,' he declared urbanely, and Emma was reduced to impotent silence as the lights dimmed and the music heralded the onset of the evening's performance.

On reflection the play was a good one, an innovative slant on an old classic, and perhaps it was as well she required total concentration to comprehend the fast-paced Italian dialogue, for it meant she could temporarily forget the forceful man at her side.

'Would you like to visit a nearby bar for an espresso coffee or cappuccino?' Nick queried as they emerged from the theatre a few hours later.

The thought of spending a further hour in his company merely flared her nerve-endings into frightening life. 'I'm rather tired,' she evinced evenly, directing her attention to the vicinity of his black bow-tie. 'And it will be an hour before we reach the villa.'

'Then we will go home.'

His voice was bland, but Emma wasn't deceived by his amenability for a minute.

Once seated in the car she leaned her head against the cushioned head-rest and watched as Nick crossed round and slid in behind the wheel, then he fired the engine and eased the powerful vehicle into the stream of traffic.

He made no effort to converse, and she concentrated her attention on the passing night scene, fascinated by the bright splashes of neon above lit shop windows, the evidence of people strolling the pavements, the number of *ristorantes* with tables and chairs placed outside for patrons to sit at in relaxed enjoyment.

After a while she closed her eyes, lulled by the smooth purr of the engine and the lateness of the hour.

Emma woke with a start, unsure for a brief second what had disturbed her and equally unsure where she was. Then reality surfaced, and she became aware the Ferrari was stationary inside the garage. Was it a figment of her imagination, or had something brushed her temple?

Of their own volition her lashes swept upward and she met Nick's inimical gaze. Light reflected from the ceiling filtered into the car's interior and lent angles to his strong features, making it difficult to judge anything from his expression.

A tiny pulse quickened at the base of her throat and began to hammer in palpable confusion as he made no move to vacate his seat, and she wanted to run as fast as she could, yet *stay*. As crazy as it seemed, she wanted, *needed* to feel the strength of his arms, the touch of his mouth on hers, to be swept high on a tide of sensation that would ease the deep, aching void within.

It would take only the slightest gesture on her part, and there would be no turning back. She could see it in his eyes, sense it in the coiled tenseness of his body, the intent watchfulness apparent.

Even as she hesitated, a feeling of self-disgust washed over her, and she reached for the door handle, then slipped out from the car to stand waiting as he secured the garage.

Tension filled the air until it assumed a highly volatile quality, and her stomach muscles clenched in painful reaction as he crossed to her side.

A quick glance was all that was needed to witness Nick's narrowed scrutiny and the latent anger evident, and Emma felt a surge of blazing rage at her own stupidity in permitting him to get beneath her skin. The private battle she'd been waging for days against recognition of her emotions rose damnably to the surface, bringing guilt and self-loathing to a degree where she wanted to lash out at the one person responsible—hurt him as much as she was hurting.

'Leave me alone!' The words emerged as an anguished whisper the instant he caught hold of her elbow, and he swore briefly, explicitly, as his gaze raked her slender frame. 'I'm not a child in need of a restraining hand!'

'I was merely offering gentlemanly assistance,' Nick drawled, and her answering laugh came out sounding slightly off-key.

'Is that what you call it? Why, then, do I feel positively *shackled*?'

All of a sudden his presence was a definite threat in the semi-darkness, and she was supremely conscious of their surroundings, the dimly lit path leading through the garden and the lateness of the hour.

'Were you such a shrew with Marc?'

The query threw her off balance, and she looked at him with pain-filled eyes. 'No,' she denied unsteadily. 'We never argued.'

One eyebrow rose in sardonic cynicism. 'My dear Emma, *never*?' His eyes gleamed darkly with latent amusement. 'No outbursts that were healed with the sweetness of making up?'

'What would you have me do? Invent some arguments

just for your satisfaction?' she vented, endeavouring to control her temper. 'Marc was kind and thoughtful, and willing to do anything to please.'

He regarded her solemnly for several long seconds, then he remarked quietly, 'You argue with me.'

'Because you rub me up the wrong way!' she cried, sorely tried.

'Have you given a thought to *why*?'

'*Yes*, damn you!'

'And you don't like it,' he drawled imperturbably, his eyes watchfully intent.

'You're damned right, I don't!' Her anger had whipped itself into such a fine fury that her eyes sparkled with brilliant fire, making them appear like crystallised topaz.

'Such vehemence,' Nick mocked as he conducted a slow, encompassing appraisal, lingering on the agitated pulse-beat at the base of her throat, the deepness of her eyes and their dilation, the soft, trembling mouth. He lifted a hand and let his fingers trail down her left cheek. 'Why not take it one day at a time,' he suggested tolerantly, 'without attempting to analyse and pin down every provoking emotion?'

Her chin lifted fractionally. 'Is a degree in psychology one of your attributes?'

'What a delightful mixture you are,' he accorded musingly 'One minute a termagant, the next a polite child.'

Resentment flared, sharpening her tongue. 'You bring out the worst in me,' she retorted, and became incensed when he laughed.

Without thought her hand flew in a swift arc towards

his face, and the resounding slap sounded loud in the silence of the garden.

There was a brief glimpse of terrible anger in his eyes, and for a few timeless seconds she thought he meant to strike her back.

Shock kept her immobile, and as the consequences of her actions slowly penetrated her brain she became filled with a terrible sense of shame. Never in her life had she been so moved to anger, nor had there been a moment when her normally sunny nature digressed to such an extent she'd felt impelled to hit anyone.

An apology, *any* words she could utter in excuse seemed pointless, yet convention demanded she extend them.

'I'm sorry.'

'No, you're not,' Nick opined drily, and she raised startled eyes to meet his hooded expression.

A muscle tensed along his powerful jaw, and she suddenly felt as if she was about to tread on broken glass. One false move and she would be consumed with pain. Looking at him, there was no doubt as to what form it would take.

'Please—don't,' she implored shakily, held motionless in mesmerised fascination as he leant out a hand and caught hold of her chin.

Another slid beneath the swathe of her hair to capture her nape, and her lips parted in silent protest, her eyes widening into huge pools, mirroring despair as his head lowered down to hers.

A silent moan became locked in her throat as her lips were taken, *possessed*, in a manner that was punishingly cruel, and he plundered the sweet softness of her mouth in a kiss that became a total invasion of her senses. Her jaw ached, and her tongue felt numb and swollen as he exacted retribution. Just as she thought she could stand no more, he tore his mouth away in a gesture of self-disgust.

Emma almost swayed at the sudden movement, and she clutched for the only solid entity within reach to prevent herself from falling; then realisation of the strong, muscled arms beneath her hands made her lift them away as if they'd been scorched by flame.

Her eyes seemed locked with his, their expression trapped and filled with pain, and her lips began to tremble, their movement totally beyond her control.

Without conscious thought she lifted unsteady fingers to her mouth.

A husky string of epithets assailed her ears, and she cried out as hard hands drew her close, their grip bruising the delicate bones of her shoulders as his head bent towards hers, and she closed her eyes against a further onslaught, her hands fluttering uselessly to her side as his lips brushed against her temple, then slid across first one eyelid, then the other before trailing down to rest at the edge of her mouth.

His touch was curiously gentle as he traced the swollen outline with evocative slowness, savouring the faint saltiness before dispensing it with his tongue, then with infinite care he teased her lower lip apart and she gave an incoherent groan at such flagrant seduction.

A slow warmth entered her veins as his lips travelled down the pulsing cord at the edge of her neck to begin an erotic discovery of the hollows beneath her throat, and it was only when he moved lower towards the gentle swell of her breasts that reason surfaced and with it a stark horror at what she might be inviting.

Even as she struggled, he raised his head, and Emma stood frozen, almost afraid to move. She began to tremble as she instinctively crossed her arms across her breasts, hugging them tightly in an effort to still the deep shudders that shook her slim frame.

'Why do you look at me as if I intend rape, or worse?' A muscle tautened along the edge of his jaw, and his eyes darkened with smouldering bleakness. '*Cristo!*' His voice held a dangerous softness that sent icy shivers scudding down her spine, and she was powerless to resist the pressure of his hand as he grasped hold of her chin and forced her to look at him. 'I won't deny a need to have you in my bed,' he stated with brutal frankness. 'But when it happens it will be *me* you want, *my* possession you crave.' He paused deliberately, the leashed savagery in his voice flicking over her with the stinging rawness of a whip. 'Not someone to act as a shadowy substitute for Marc.'

To her consternation her mouth began to tremble and silly, ignominious tears welled in her eyes, distorting her vision. As if from a distance she heard his harsh curse, then gentle hands pulled her into his arms and cradled her head into the curve of his shoulder.

In the darkness his features appeared carved into an expressionless mask.

'It wasn't my intention to punish you. Myself, perhaps,' he mused wryly, letting his lips tease the delicately scented curls above her forehead before putting her at arm's length. 'Come, let us go inside.'

There wasn't a single thing she could think of to say in

response, and without a word she preceded him indoors, through to the wide, curving staircase that led to the upper floor.

Emma didn't falter, uncaring whether he followed her or not, and on reaching her bedroom she closed the door behind her then crossed to subside weakly on to the bed.

Dear God! Never in her life had she evoked such leashed violence. It was almost as if some diabolical force was intent on arranging a clash so horrendous she began to wonder if it wasn't born out of Hell.

CHAPTER SIX

EMMA studiously ignored Nick over the next few days, pleading the need for a rest from sightseeing, and expressing a desire to relax at the villa itself in order to spend more time with Rosa.

The gardens were alive with a variety of flowers and shrubs creating a riot of glorious colour, and Emma busied herself filling the numerous vases in the spacious foyer, the *sala* and the *salone* with freshly cut blooms.

There was a guest list to compile, Rosa told her, for the party she and Enzo intended giving on Saturday evening, and a menu to be selected.

Together they talked, reminiscing over the elderly couple's annual visits to Australia, the good times they'd all shared. And Marc. If Rosa suspected Emma's friendship with Nick was becoming more than platonic she sagely kept her own counsel, and Emma avoided even mentioning his name.

Each morning Nick retired with Enzo into the study to explore the intricacies of the financial world and, as Rosa laughingly indicated, to test each other's mental skill.

Annalisa busied herself writing letters to friends and her favourite boarding-school tutor, Sister Margherita, played tennis with her father and, on occasion, Emma, and sought to improve her butterfly stroke in the swimming pool.

During the evenings they watched television or played

a friendly game of cards, then relaxed over coffee before retiring to bed.

A drive through the Alban Hills was arranged for Friday, and Emma rose early, then showered. She selected a cool white jumpsuit with the trouser cuffs rolled several inches above her ankles, a deep aquamarine belt at her waist and matching sandals, then she applied sunscreen cream and covered it with minimum make-up. The result was one of casual elegance and, satisfied with her appearance, she made her way downstairs to the *sala* where she helped herself to fresh criossants and plum conserve.

Nick entered the room just as she was finishing her coffee, and she felt the tension begin to manifest itself inside her stomach, tightening her nerves into a painful knot.

It was useless to curse and rage against fate; equally impossible at the eleventh hour to invent a plausible excuse and opt out.

His presence created havoc and, attired in casual, dark blue cotton trousers teamed with a matching short-sleeved shirt, he excuded dangerous masculinity from every nerve and fibre.

'Good morning.' His voice was a soft drawl, and dark eyes lanced hers, narrowing faintly as he glimpsed the defensiveness apparent. Then he crossed to the table with indolent grace and folded his lengthy frame into a nearby chair.

At once her pulse-beat began hammering in chaotic confusion, and she strove valiantly to maintain her composure as she returned his greeting.

'Are you waiting for me?'

'There is no immediate hurry,' Nick told her with a

negligible shrug. He appeared to study her, his gaze thoughtful and far too shrewd for her peace of mind. 'Annalisa will be down any minute, then we'll leave.' One eyebrow slanted in musing mockery. 'Do you want more coffee?'

Her eyes flashed golden sparks, then became veiled as she deliberately lowered her lashes. 'Is that a polite reminder to suggest you join me?'

'Do you imagine I need an invitation?'

A frisson of inexplicable apprehension feathered its way through her body at the unwarranted implication, and she declined to answer.

At that moment the door opened and Rosa entered the room. 'Good morning, Emma. Nick.' Her gaze moved from the slim auburn-haired girl to her nephew, sensing the electric tension apparent and choosing to ignore it. 'I trust you both slept well?'

'Yes, thank you,' Emma responded with undue politeness. A downright lie, but it was hardly to her advantage to admit the truth. Summoning a smile, she excused herself lightly. 'I'll just put the finishing touches to my make-up and collect my bag. I won't be long.'

If she'd had a choice she would have elected to sit next to Annalisa in the rear of the car, but any thoughts she might have entertained in that direction were quelled in an instant by the implacability evident in Nick's expression as he held open the front passenger door and saw her into her seat.

The sky was a clear azure, and at this early hour the sun's heat had yet to reveal its intense beat. Beneath Nick's drawling commentary they explored the charming Alban Hill towns where vineyards on the slopes above Lake Albano and Lake Nemi were purported to produce most of the white wine consumed in Rome.

'Marino, Rocca de Papa and Frascati are famous for their grape-harvest festivals in the autumn,' Nick relayed, and Emma gazed at the neat rows of vines with their plump grapes almost ready for picking. There were white and pink splashed houses, some fresh-painted and others which bore an aged sienna hue.

All told, it was an artist's dream, and one which she couldn't help but admire. 'It's beautiful,' she stated simply, unwilling to accord the exotic, but startlingly rustic scenery with extravagant superlatives.

'The lakes are splendid,' Nick murmured gently, sparing her a warm, musing glance. 'We will stop further on and visit one of the vineyards where it is possible to sample wine direct from the barrel.'

There was an element of shared intimacy, something that went beyond apparent friendliness. The man projected an aura of quiet strength and indomitable will; a lethal mixture of silk and steel from which escape was becoming increasingly more difficult.

Maybe she should just give in and allow him to lead her in whichever direction he chose, without thought for anything other than *now*.

Yet something held her back, some intrinsic element of integrity that baulked at acting in such a capricious fashion, even in today's era, where selective promiscuity was the norm. And deep down she was afraid. Afraid the dreams and esteem interwoven with her memory of Marc might crumble into obscurity beneath the sensuality and sexual expertise of the man who wanted to usurp his place.

With determined effort Emma dragged her mind back to the present and concentrated her attention on the scene beyond the windscreen. The views were breathtaking, with wooded hills providing a startling contrast with the deep blue of the lakes. It was a glorious vista of vivid colour, and she gave a small gasp of surprise when Nick pointed out a ruined castle and acquiesced with indulgence when Annalisa begged if they could stop so she could explore it.

'Of course.' He brought the car to a halt and slid out from behind the wheel, then crossed round to open the passenger door.

The ruins were a mixture of rubble and outer walls, with some evidence of apportioned rooms. There was a feeling of unreality walking the same ground that emperors and soldiers had trod several centuries before. If one closed one's eyes it was almost possible to imagine the clanking of swords and the rollicking laughter of the Sybarites.

Back in the car, Nick drove for several kilometres, then stopped within sight of Lake Albano so they could have a picnic lunch.

Annalisa helped spread the checked cloth on the grassy bank beneath the spreading branches of a shady tree, then chattered innocuously as Nick extracted the hamper from the boot and deposited it within easy reach.

'Lovely!' the young girl exclaimed as she began unpacking an assortment of covered containers. 'Maria has packed chicken and ham, two kinds of salad, some fruit and lots of fresh-baked crusty bread rolls.'

'And wine,' Nick smiled, retrieving a bottle from its cooled container. He selected three glasses and filled one with lemonade for his daughter, then poured wine into the remaining two, handing one to Emma before lifting his own in a silent salute.

'What will you have, Emma?' Annalisa asked as she busied herself with plates and cutlery.

'I'll help you.'

Dividing the food, she passed one plate to Nick, another to Annalisa, then placed a small selection on to her own.

'Isn't this *nice*?' Annalisa grinned engagingly as she bit into her chicken leg. 'What are you going to wear for the party, Emma?' Her eyes became round with intense interest. 'Zia Rosa and Zio Enzo always have grand parties. The ladies wear masses of jewellery and try to outdo each other. And very important people come. Don't they, *Papa*?'

'Indeed they do, *piccina*,' Nick agreed gently. 'Zio Enzo is a very clever financial entepreneur who maintains an active interest in several business ventures.'

'Just like you,' his daughter agreed solemnly. She finished her chicken and filled a split roll with slices of ham, then munched it appreciatively before washing it all down with lemonade. 'I think,' she declared, standing to her feet with graceful agility, 'I will go and pick some flowers to take back to Zia Rosa.'

'They may not stay fresh for long inside the car,' Nick warned, only to recieve a blithe smile in return.

'But water will revive them, and besides, Zia won't mind. It is the thought that counts.'

Emma lifted her glass and sipped its contents, unsure whether Annalisa had deliberately contrived an excuse in order to leave the two adults on their own.

'More chicken?'

She glanced up and met Nick's gleaming gaze. 'No, thanks.'

'Wine?'

Shaking her head in silent negation she placed her empty plate down on to the checked cloth and selected a paper napkin to wipe her fingers.

Sitting so close, she could see the tiny lines fanning out from the edge of his eyes, sense their clear, unwavering regard for an infinitesimal second before she lowered her eyes to the deep grooves slashing each cheek. She hadn't meant to look at his mouth, but her eyes were drawn to the sensual curve of their own volition. Her pulse tripped its beat and gathered speed until she could feel it pounding at the base of her throat.

'I think I'll go and help Annalisa,' she declared unevenly, and he looked at her with a steady regard, holding her gaze for what seemed an age.

'Do I pose such a threat that you must run away?'

His words jolted her composure, and in the need to retain it she blurted out, 'Threat?' Her voice sounded husky and strangely vulnerable. 'You'd have to be impossibly arrogant to suppose that.'

'*Impossibly*, Emma?'

A prickle of apprehension slithered icily down to the base of her spine, warning her to desist before she found herself engaged in a verbal battle. He had the most damnable way of deploying words, calculated without doubt to pull her off balance.

'I'm in no position to judge,' she returned evenly, determined not to give him the satisfaction of rousing her to anger.

'Would you like to be?'

Even as she registered the implication of his words, a silent, screaming refusal roared through her brain, almost deafening in its volume. 'No.'

His soft laughter sent a multitude of sensations

spiralling through her body, and before she had a chance to move he reached forward and brushed his lips against her cheek; then his mouth fastened over hers in a kiss that was brief and punishingly hard.

'That wasn't fair,' she accused him shakily, silently hating him. She almost died when his head descended once more, although this time there was a wealth of seduction in his touch, a gentleness that was bewitchingly sensual as his lips caressed hers, settling with unerring ease over their delicate curves, savouring, tasting in a manner that made her gasp with outraged indignation.

Too late she realised her mistake, for his mouth became demanding, possessive as he invaded the soft inner sweetness to create a ravishment of her senses.

Slowly, he began a deliberately flagrant exploration before slipping to nuzzle the delicate hollows at the base of her throat. Next, he trailed the pulsing cord at the edge of her neck up to her earlobe before slipping across to reclaim her mouth.

Emma was melting inside, warmth slowly encompassing her body, sending the blood coursing through her veins until her whole being was consumed by a deep, throbbing awareness. She dimly registered Nick's quick, indrawn breath before his mouth hardened, its pressure becoming relentless as he plundered at will, introducing her to a degree of sensual mastery she hadn't dreamed existed.

Emma became conscious of an almost mindless ecstasy that combined a beautiful melding of sheer sensation with elusive alchemy, and she experienced a terrible sense of loss as he gently disentangled her arms and released her.

She could only look at him as gentle fingers lifted her

chin, and her lashes swiftly lowered as he traced the outline of her trembling mouth. Pride alone was responsible for the way she slowly let her lashes sweep upwards to focus on a point slightly beneath his eyes.

'That shouldn't have happened.'

'Why ever not?' Nick queried gently. 'We shared a few kisses, that was all.'

All? If his kisses affected her so tumultuously, how could she cope with his lovemaking? She felt helplessly out of her depth, unable and unwilling to say anything that would highlight the complex state of her emotions. At last, when the silence between them seemed to have stretched into an eternity, she rose slowly to her feet and began tidying their picnic things back into the hamper.

Nick helped her, and by the time everything was stowed in the boot Annalisa had returned carrying an armful of flowers which were reverently placed in damp newspaper in the boot.

They headed north for a number of kilometres to a nearby village where Nick indicated they would stop to sample wine in one of the many vineyards dotted across the meandering hillside.

'A small family establishment which has been handed down from generation to generation,' he explained as he drew the car into the courtyard and brought it to a halt in front of an aged stone house. 'Their claim to fame is an excellent vintage dry white, the fermentation process being a closely guarded secret known only to selected family members,' he revealed as they walked towards the cellars.

They were welcomed with enthusiastic conviviality, and Emma accepted a glass of wine and sipped it tentatively, surprised to find the bouquet was exceptional, the taste sharp to her relatively untutored palate.

'Excellent,' Nick declared, letting his gaze sweep towards Emma. 'Don't you think so?'

'Yes.' Even so, she couldn't finish it, and after a few minutes he took the glass from her hand and with a gesture that was vaguely intimate he lifted it to his lips and drained the contents in one long swallow.

She looked at him in surprise, glimpsing the warmth apparent in the depths of his eyes, and she was unable to prevent the agonising shaft of sensation that slowly unfurled inside her stomach. Then Annalisa drew her attention to the huge barrels of wine lined up against one wall, and she dragged her thoughts away from the compelling man at her side.

It was almost seven o'clock when they returned to the villa, and after sharing a cool drink in the *salone*, during which Annalisa imparted a résumé of their day for Rosa's benefit, Emma excused herself and made her way upstairs to shower and change before dinner.

Rosa and Enzo's party promised to be a glittering formal affair, and Emma dressed with care.

The dress she'd elected to wear was a deep cobalt-blue silk with draped bodice, delicate straps and a softly draped skirt that flowed with every movement she made. Slim-heeled shoes completed the outfit, and she viewed her mirrored reflection with detached satisfaction before selecting a diamond and sapphire pendant and matching earstuds from her jewellery case; then she clipped on a bracelet that had formed part of her wedding gift from Marc.

There were only the final touches of her make-up to attend to, and she chose to highlight her eyes with a careful blending of shadow and mascara, then added a thin film of gloss over her lipstick. Givenchy's *L'Interdit* was her favourite perfume, and she sprayed the atomiser generously over the valley between her breasts, at her nape, the hollows at the base of her throat, her wrists and ankles before giving her appearance one final scrutiny in the cheval-glass mirror.

A slim, attractive-looking young woman gazed solemnly back, and Emma smiled, pleased with her total look. She was armed and ready to do battle with the indomitable Nick Castelli, and any other male guests who might attempt to indulge in a harmless flirtation!

A slight mirthless laugh escaped her lips. There was nothing *harmless* about Nick. His resolve to infiltrate her emotions was nothing less than daunting, and it took every ounce of courage to turn and walk calmly down the stairs.

'Ah, there you are,' Annalisa declared with delight as Emma entered the *salone*, and her warm, hazel eyes glowed with genuine admiration. 'You look beautiful. Doesn't she, *Papa*?'

'Indeed she does,' Nick agreed appreciatively, and Emma met his dark, enigmatic gaze with equanimity.

'Thank you,' she returned gracefully. The sight of him attired in a dark, formal evening suit did strange things to her equilibrium, and she accepted the glass of wine Enzo proffered, sipping its contents in the vain hope that alcohol might restore some sense of calm.

There had to be some sane, logical reason for the way he affected her, surely? Perhaps it was quite normal to wonder what it would be like to sleep with another man? To be able to compare . . . No! Her mind screeched to a shuddering halt at such a wayward train of thought. Oh

God, what was happening to her? Instead of getting better, it was becoming worse with every passing day. If she didn't leave Italy soon, she'd go completely mad!

'Emma! How lovely you look!'

She turned slightly and a generous smile curved her lips. 'Thank you, Rosa. Is there anything I can do to help?'

'No, *cara*,' the older woman responded warmly. 'However, there are a few friends who are waiting for an introduction. Will you come and meet them?'

Two hours and two glasses of wine later Emma was convinced her face had assumed a masklike quality from projecting polite congeniality to a number of people it was unlikely she'd ever see again after tonight.

There were approximately fifty guests mingling in the luxuriously appointed *salone*, and she registered the lilt of subdued chatter at the same moment she caught sight of a familiar dark head apparently engaged in conversation with, of all people, Danielle Fabrese.

Emma's stomach performed a painful somersault, then settled down to a dull ache as her already tautened nerves stretched to breaking point. Somehow she doubted Danielle had been invited on her own account. It was far more likely the model had ingratiated herself as a partner to one of Rosa and Enzo's bona fide guests.

At that moment Nick glanced up and Emma met his intent gaze with a slight lift of her chin and a hint of coolness in the depths of her gold eyes.

'Emma. Let me fetch you another drink.'

She turned towards the owner of that friendly voice and gave Vince such a stunning smile he looked visibly taken aback for an instant. Then his teeth gleamed and a silent laugh parted his lips.

'Ah, I see,' he mocked lightly. 'You want to use me as a foil to get back at Nick!'

'Not at all,' she disclaimed quietly. 'You're a very pleasant young man whose company I happen to enjoy.'

'And Danielle, deep in conversation with Nick, has nothing to do with it?'

'No,' she said firmly, willing it to be true as she attempted to ignore a tiny gremlin who suddenly materialised inside her head and whispered 'Liar!' in a deliberate taunt.

A waiter paused discreetly, and Vince took two glasses from the tray, one of which he offered Emma.

'Hmm, gorgeous,' he murmured softly. 'Your perfume alone could drive a man wild.'

It was impossible not to laugh at such blatant flattery, and a winsome smile curved Emma's generous mouth. 'Careful,' she cautioned. 'I might take you seriously.'

'I should be so fortunate.'

'What of Danielle?' she reminded him, wrinkling her nose at him in silent admonition, and caught his faint grimace.

'A pretty playmate, nothing more, who shamelessly uses me in an effort to get close to my inestimable cousin.' His smile broadened as he glimpsed her expression. 'I have no illusions about Danielle,' he continued wryly, 'whereas you, Emma, are a sweet young woman. Nick thinks so, too, and Annalisa already adores you.'

'Your cousin has been very helpful,' she answered carefully. 'I've appreciated the time he has spared me.'

'And you are just "good friends", hmm?' Vince mocked.

Anyone further removed from *friend* was difficult to imagine, yet she was loath to pursue the subject. 'I don't think I have to answer that.'

'Ah, astute,' he concluded sardonically, sparing her a whimsical smile. 'Astute enough, I wonder, to realise that Nick has a reputation for getting what he wants? And——' he paused with soft deliberation, then added, 'my guess favours *you*, sweet Emma.'

Her heart gave a sudden lurch, then settled back to its normal pattern as she endeavoured a semblance of tranquillity in the face of Vince's revelation.

'If the studied ease with which Nick has been regarding us for the past five minutes is any indication, you don't stand a chance in hell of escaping him.'

She met his gaze inflinchingly. 'He doesn't own me.'

'Not yet,' he corrected softly.

'Not ever!'

'Such vehemence,' he chided musingly. 'I am almost inclined to think you protest too much.'

'You're wrong,' Emma assured quickly, tempering her words with a smile.

Vince reminded her so much of Marc, and she experienced a strange, inexplicable pang of sadness, intermingled with the knowledge that soon she would have to return to her memories, face again her parents, Marc's, and various friends. Say goodbye to the overpowering Nick Castelli, whose motives she failed to understand.

'Talk of the devil,' Vince murmured, and Emma turned slowly to see Nick weaving his way steadily towards them.

It was impossible to discern anything from his expression, and she offered him a slight smile as he reached her side.

'Would you prefer mineral water?' Nick enquired,

glancing at her barely touched wine.

'No, thank you,' she responded evenly, hating the faint tremor that ran through her body in reaction to his close promixity. His slight smile drew attention to his mouth, and remembering the way it felt to have him kiss her brought a rush of colour to her cheeks.

'Something to eat?'

She bore his probing scrutiny equably, and gave a negative shake of her head. 'Maybe later.'

The depths of his eyes assumed a degree of lazy tolerance. 'You wouldn't by any chance have decided to be perverse and deliberately oppose me?'

'What makes you think that?'

His gaze narrowed and assumed an inscrutability, a watchfulness that was somehow worse than any patronising amusement.

'Perhaps you resented me talking to Danielle and decided to reciprocate by flirting with Vince?'

Her chin lifted fractionally at the unfairness of such a supposition, and she directed him a cool glare. 'I did *not* flirt! Besides, Vince is uncomplicated, and nice.'

'While I am not.'

What could she say? Anything would be equally damning, so she chose silence for what seemed for ever before saying slowly, 'I'm very grateful to you for making my stay in Rome so interesting.'

'Very politely spoken,' he declared cynically.

'You doubt my sincerity?'

'No.'

'*Papa*, have you told Emma yet?'

The sound of Annalisa's voice brought some semblance of normality to their conversation, and Emma moved slightly to allow Annalisa to join them.

'I am so looking forward to driving to Naples next week,' the young girl enthused, clearly excited at the prospect. 'Emma will adore it, won't she, *Papa*?' She turned towards Emma and caught hold of her hand. 'They say "see Naples and die". The scenery is magnificent, and as for Capri—I love it there.'

Somehow Emma managed to school her features and offer a pleasant comment, wondering if there was any chance she could invent some excuse and not go.

'I haven't had the opportunity to discuss it with Emma yet, *piccina*. She may have other plans.'

The disappointment on his daughter's face was plainly evident as she looked at Emma. 'But you *must* come with us! It won't be the same if you don't.'

Diplomacy was the only way to deal with the situation, and Emma gently squeezed Annalisa's hand. 'Can I think about it and let your father know?'

'Yes, of course.'

Emma felt her heart turn over at the girl's quiet resignation, and she almost relented and said she would accept. Dammit, why did she feel so—wretched? The choice to refuse should be hers without the need for guilt at doing so.

'Will you excuse me for a few minutes?' She put her glass down on a nearby table and made her way from the *salone* with the intention of freshening her make-up.

The powder room placed at the guests' disposal was adjacent the foyer on the ground floor, and Emma was about to enter it when the door was opened from the inside and she came face to face with Danielle, who, instead of emerging, elected to retrace her steps.

'Perhaps I could re-touch my lipstick,' Danielle murmured with a false smile, and Emma mentally prepared herself for a verbal onslaught without the slightest doubt to whom it would pertain.

'Nice strategy, *cara*. Inveigling an invitation to the villa at the time when Nick is here with his daughter.' Her eyes were glittery and strangely avid, and Emma endeavoured to remain calm beneath the model's intent stare.

'I had no idea,' she assured Danielle evenly, crossing to the marble basin. Via mirrored reflection she glimpsed Danielle's expression and saw one eyebrow arch delicately in disbelief.

'Next you will tell me Rosa and Enzo neglected to inform you of Nick's existence.'

Emma lifted a hand to her hair and smoothed back a few stray curls, then she pretended to scrutinise her make-up. 'They probably did mention him at some time during their visits to Sydney, but I can't honestly remember.'

'And this holiday in Rome *now* is merely coincidence, and not specifically contrived to ensnare Nick——' A tinkling laugh full of bitterness emerged from her lips. '—who has to be much bigger fish than your sadly departed husband, surely?' Her eyes assumed a malevolent gleam as she thrust in for the verbal kill. 'So much better, when considering re-marriage, to keep it in the family? Especially when the lineage is affiliated to the rich and powerful Martinero dynasty.'

'I think this has gone far enough, don't you?' Emma managed quietly, sure that she couldn't cope with any futher disparaging invective. It had been bad enough listening to Vince's light, bantering innuendo without compouding it further.

'Nick Castelli is going to be mine,' Danielle declared

viciously. 'Do you understand?'

Emma looked at the model and tried to be objective. 'I understand, Danielle,' she said evenly. 'But do you? If you have known Nick for so long, why isn't he already yours?' She let her eyes sweep slowly over Danielle's superb figure. 'You are very beautiful, except,' she paused fractionally, then continued, 'in your heart, where it really matters. A fact which Nick has obviously recognised, wouldn't you say?'

For a moment Emma thought Danielle meant to launch a physical attack, and she braced herself in an attempt to ward off the sudden push that spun her back against the marble pedestal.

'*Bitch!*'

Danielle turned and swept from the room, and Emma was left to shakily gather herself sufficiently together in order to rejoin the other guests and attempt to pretend none of this had happened.

Something, she perceived several long minutes later, it would take considerable effort and no mean feat of acting ability to achieve.

CHAPTER SEVEN

'MAY I join you?'

Emma glanced up and met Vince's gleaming gaze as he leaned forward and bestowed a light kiss to Rosa's cheek.

'Lovely party, Zia Rosa,' he said gently.

'Thank you, Vince,' Rosa accepted warmly. 'Emma and I were discussing a visit to the galleries one day next week.'

'What a pity I must be in Milan until Sunday,' he declared with sincere regret. 'Otherwise it would give me pleasure to accompany you.'

The slight nagging ache at the back of her eyes had begun within ten minutes of the scene with Danielle, and had intensified over the past hour until it bore all the symptoms of a migraine. A regrettable legacy from last year's car accident, although admittedly they recurred with less frequency. A deep, throbbing sensation manifested itself at one temple and threatened to overwhelm her with pain, and she cursed beneath her breath. If she didn't swallow some tablets soon, she'd have little option but to take to her bed. Prescribed medication combined with half an hour's rest might alleviate the worst of it, and with luck her absence wouldn't even be noticed, she decided as she quietly informed Rosa of her intention.

'Oh, Emma, I am so sorry.' Rosa sympathised at once, her kindly features creased with concern. 'You do look very pale. Are you sure you will be all right?'

'Quite sure,' she declared, attempting a smile, except it didn't quite come off and merely ended up as a wobbly substitute. 'Don't worry, I'll be fine.' Excusing herself, she turned and threaded her way through the milling guests to the staircase, and once in her bedroom she stripped off her dress, slipped out of her shoes and donned a silk wrap. Then she extracted two tablets and washed them down with water before laying down on the bed.

The darkened room was bliss after the electric brightness of the *salone*, and Emma closed her eyes and willed the pain to subside.

What had triggered it off this time? she brooded wearily. Perhaps it was a culmination of several factors, not the least of which was Nick Castelli.

Dammit, she'd felt so *safe* with Marc, so sure, even in grief, of what her future would entail. She had a fascinating, fulfilling career, and there were numerous friends available whenever she needed a social partner. She didn't *need* an involvement with any man, much less one who resided on the opposite side of the world.

A slight sound alerted her attention and she slowly let her eyelids drift open to focus on a slight figure standing hesitantly beside the bed.

'Emma? Zia Rosa said I could come and see if you are feeling any better.'

'A little,' Emma responded cautiously.

'Is it very bad?' Annalisa whispered with concerned awe. 'I have never had a headache before.'

She couldn't help the faint smile that parted her lips. 'Pray that you never do. At least, nothing as dramatic as a migraine.'

'Can I get Maria to bring you some tea, or a cool drink?'

'A cup of tea would be lovely, *piccina*,' she declared, unconsciously using Nick's pet name for the young girl.

'It might help.' Annalisa ventured, and Emma lifted a hand in silent agreement.

'Thank you.'

Annalisa crept from the room, and Emma closed her eyes against the misting pain. Already she felt heavy and vaguely disorientated as the tablets began to take effect. If only she could sleep, even briefly. An hour would be sufficient, then she'd wake feeling considerably refreshed.

It was some time later that she became aware someone had entered the room, and she sensed rather than heard their passage towards the bed. Then there was a faint click as the bedside lamp sprang on, and she gave a faint murmur of distress at the sudden intrusion of light.

'Please—that hurts my eyes,' she protested, and gave a slight sigh of relief when it was switched off and the light in the adjoining bathroom provided a subdued and slightly removed illumination.

'Just put the cup on the pedestal. I'll drink it soon.'

'Unless you have a penchant for lukewarm tea, I would advise drinking it now,' a deep, all too familiar voice drawled.

Emma's eyes opened to centre on the man standing indolently near the bed.

'What are you doing here?' It wasn't really a query, merely a shocked acknowledgment of his presence in her bedroom.

'You're quite safe,' Nick murmured with deceptive

softness, and she felt the prick of futile tears at his implication.

I don't *feel* safe, she longed to scream at him.

'Rosa showed concern over your welfare,' he continued quietly. 'And Annalisa showed considerable alarm. I deemed it wise to check for myself.'

'I've already taken two tablets,' she managed wearily. 'So your solicitude, although—gratifying, is unnecessary.' A spasm of pain seemed to focus itself behind one eye, and she winced.

'You really do have a headache,' Nick declared with a brooding frown, and she felt every muscle in her body tense with reaction as he folded his length down on to the edge of the bed.

'What did you imagine?' she flung at him tiredly. 'That I invented the excuse solely to escape your diabolical presence?'

'The thought did occur.' Lifting a hand, he touched his fingers to her temple. 'There?'

Emma closed her eyes against the effect he was having on her, and she willed her pulse to steady from its sudden leaping beat as he began a gentle, soothing massage, using the tips of his fingers to probe out the pain and attempt to alleviate it.

There was an element of danger in permitting him to continue, for the seducing quality of his touch played havoc with her senses, making her all too aware of just how easy it would be to succumb. All she had to do was lift her arms and let her hands encircle his neck, pull his head down to hers and allow herself to be swept away on a tide of emotion.

'Is that any better?'

Emma slowly opened her eyes and almost died at the

intense awareness evident in his dark gaze. 'Yes. Thanks,' she added unsteadily, more as an afterthought than in gratitude. Her lashes swept down, veiling the bruised darkness in her eyes.

'Do you get these attacks often?'

His voice seemed to invade her body, and she shivered at its traitorous compliance.

'They have become less frequent,' she answered quietly. 'The doctor assures they will gradually fade altogether after the first year.'

'You suffered concussion at the time of the accident?'

'Yes.'

'Sit up and drink your tea,' Nick instructed gently, sliding an arm beneath her shoulders as he lifted her to lean back against the pillow.

Obediently she sipped from the cup, then when it was empty he replaced it down on to the pedestal.

'You resemble a lost little waif,' Nick remarked with a twisted smile. 'All eyes, pale skin, and infinitely fragile.'

'And you, Nick? What role do you play? That of my protector?'

Her eyes widened measurably when he leaned forward and lightly caressed her lips with his own. It was an evocative gesture, and one which left her aching for more.

'It would take an utter brute to be anything else.' A smile curved his wide mouth, and a gleam of amusement lit his eyes.

'I think you'd better go.' Was that her voice? She felt like a disembodied spectator, watching a scene unfold in which she had no living part.

'As soon as you have settled down for the night.' He moved the pillow back into its original position and straightened the sheet. 'Rosa gave me strict instructions that you were to stay where you are.'

She opened her mouth to protest, only to have him press his fingers fleetingly against her lips.

'No arguments. Where do you keep your nightgown?'

A strangled gasp emerged in outraged indignation. 'I'll change just as soon as you leave.'

'*Now*, Emma.' He was smiling, but there was an inflexible quality in his voice that commanded compliance. 'You should realise I am quite capable of carrying out the task myself, if you refuse.'

Stupid, mutinous tears brimmed to the surface and threatened to spill over and run down her cheeks.

'Sweet Mother of God, don't cry,' he berated huskily.

'I'm not. I just can't handle you any more.' One solitary tear escaped and trickled slowly down to rest at the edge of her mouth. 'At least, not tonight.'

Something darkened in the depths of those obsidian eyes for a brief second before vanishing beneath a mask of inscrutability. 'Will it make you feel better if I retreat into the hallway for the necessary few minutes it takes you to change?'

'I'm not a child you need to check up on,' she voiced, immeasurably hurt.

'Indulge me, *cara*.'

Without a further word he stood to his feet and vacated the room, and Emma gingerly slid off the bed, then reached beneath her pillow for the thin slither of nylon and lace that comprised her nightwear.

It took two minutes to slip out of her wrap and remove her slip and panties; a further three to don her nightgown and scrub her face free from any traces of make-up.

She emerged from the bathroom just as Nick re-entered the bedroom, and she stood still, frozen into immobility beneath his swift, raking appraisal.

'Get into bed,' he bade gently. 'Then I'll leave.'

Her eyes were held and captured by his, and she couldn't have looked away if her life had depended on it. The tenuous hold she had on her temper strengthened with every passing second, and her tawny eyes turned liquid gold in visible defiance at his high-handedness.

'Don't,' he warned in a voice that sounded vaguely like silk being cut by razor-sharp steel, 'even think about it.'

Without looking at him she crossed to the bed and slid in between the sheets. 'Satisfied?' It was a taunt she couldn't resist, and his eyes glittered with sardonic cynicism.

'No.'

For a brief, horrifying second she thought she'd pushed him too far, and she watched in mesmerised fascination as he crossed to the bed.

Bending low, he leaned forward and grazed his lips against her own. 'Sweet Emma, how lovely you are.' His smile was gentle, softening his rugged features and dispelling much of the compelling formidability apparent.

Stay with me, she wanted to beg. Supplant Marc's ghost with a living entity, and ease this terrible need. Yet even as the words whispered silently through her brain, her body began to recoil in rejection, and she shivered, hating her traitorous flesh for craving Nick's possession.

It was almost as if every sane, sensible thought had fled, the moral convictions she'd held in such high esteem dismissed as if they were of no consequence.

Like someone emerging from a dream, she became

aware of the warm sensuality of his fingers as they traced the outline of her mouth.

'Nick——' She broke off, her eyes huge golden pools as she silently implored him to leave.

'Shh, be quiet,' he remonstrated softly as he caressed her mouth with his own, tantalising with an evocative sensuality she found almost impossible to resist. Then he raised his head with obvious reluctance, and his eyes were warm with an infinite degree of intimacy as he got to his feet.

'Goodnight, Emma. Sleep well.'

She watched him cross the room and reach for the doorknob, then he was gone, and she released her breath slowly, hardly conscious that she'd been holding it. Oh, God! She closed her eyes against his forceful features, hating the turmoil he was able to evoke without any seeming effort at all.

No matter how hard she tried, she failed to bring Marc's image easily to mind. Another vied for supremacy, his strong, masculine features an arresting, primitive force that could not be easily cast to one side.

Emotions she'd never thought to experience rose damnably to the surface, demanding recognition. Passion, in its most dangerous form. Tormenting, torturing—a bittersweet agony of the flesh. Somehow she'd identified love as encompassing that volatile emotion. Now she knew they could be separate, without any linking connection.

If fate has been a tangible entity, she could have raged against it, she decided vengefully as she fought sleep and lost, slipping into a deep medication-induced somnolence that imprisoned her until well into the following morning.

Emma rose feeling refreshed, all traces of her headache gone, and she emerged downstairs to discover from Rosa that Nick was ensconced in Enzo's study prior to the imminent arrival of an associate from London, whose fleeting visit to Rome would require much of Nick's time over the next forty-eight hours.

It was a relief to be free of his disturbing presence, and when, the following morning, Rosa suggested they should spend the day shopping, Emma agreed with alacrity, for there were a few gifts she wanted to buy for her parents and friends. Together with Annalisa they set off early, in an attempt to beat the worst of the heat.

By the end of the day they were pleasantly weary and only too glad to slip into the waiting car and be driven back to the villa by Carlo.

Showered and rested they met in the *salone* for a relaxing aperitif before adjourning to the *sala* for dinner.

Nick was unable to join them, due, Enzo revealed almost apologetically, to a business appointment which would encompass dinner and most of the evening.

Emma wondered darkly if a feminine companion formed any part of his plans, and assured herself that she didn't care if his dinner was a bona fide business engagement or otherwise.

However, even imagining him sharing an intimate evening with another woman brought forth a gamut of unenviable feelings, not the least of which she was reluctant to admit as being jealousy.

To successfully alleviate the wayward trend of her thoughts she threw herself into a bright *divertissement* regarding the merits of several different designers, discovering some hours later, to her utter surprise, that they had progressed through dinner, partaken coffee, and were comfortably seated in the *salone* without her being aware of the passage of time.

'It's quite late,' Emma declared with a degree of disbelief as Rosa stood to her feet.

'Indeed it is, my dear. I think we should retire.' Her eyes kindled with affection as they took in Emma's slightly flushed features. 'Tomorrow you drive to Naples, and Nick will doubtless want to make an early start in the morning.'

Of course! She had temporarily put it to the back of her mind, although Annalisa had mentioned the trip several times during the day, ecstatic that Emma had agreed to accompany them, after all.

Together they walked towards the foyer and mounted the staircase, bade each other goodnight at its head, then they moved in opposite directions towards their own suites.

Emma undressed and slid into bed, to lie staring sightlessly at the room's darkness for what seemed hours before slipping into a restless doze from which she woke to discover that the luminous hands of her bedside clock pointed to the witching hour of midnight instead of nearly dawn, as she had hoped.

Damn! She'd never felt less like sleep in her life. Perhaps if she went down to the kitchen and heated some milk it might help. Without further thought she slid out of bed, pulled on a silk wrap, then made her way quietly downstairs.

The kitchen was large and equipped with every modern appliance available, and it took a few scant minutes to pour milk into a saucepan and heat it while she spooned sugar into a pottery mug. Filling it with milk, she carried it to a nearby table and sank into a chair.

Sipping the steaming contents with evident enjoyment she picked up a magazine and browsed through its pages, skimming over the captions until she discovered something of interest to read.

A slight sound alerted her attention and she turned slowly to see Nick standing a few feet distant.

'I can't imagine you to be waiting up for me?'

He sounded incredibly cynical, and she met his gleaming gaze steadily, despite the faint stirring of resentment deep within.

'I couldn't sleep,' she explained carefully. 'Can I get you anything?'

'*Grazie*, but no.' He lifted a hand and raked fingers through his hair, ruffling it into attractive disorder. 'I saw the light and thought it advisable to check.'

He looked tired, almost jaded, and Emma suppressed the impossible urge to smooth the tension from his forehead, loosen his tie and unbutton his shirt and bid him relax into a comfortable chair.

'How was your business dinner?'

'You sound like a wife,' he drawled, and she felt her heart constrict with pain.

Without a word she slid to her feet and crossed to the sink with her mug, then she moved towards the door.

'Emma.' He reached out and caught hold of her arm, halting her progress, and she pulled away from him, wincing slightly as the pressure increased with steel-like intensity.

'What do you want?'

'Would you believe—*you*?'

Her eyes glittered with brilliant golden fire as a

complexity of primitive emotions fought valiantly for
control. 'Do you get a kick out of trying to wear down my
resistance? Is that it?'

She shivered, despite the warm evening temperature,
and just looking at him she was made frighteningly
aware that the chemistry between them had somehow
combined to form a perilous, combustible force.

In seeming slow motion she saw his head descend, then
his mouth closed over hers in a kiss that made anything
she had experienced before pale into insignificance.
There was a wealth of seductive mastery in his touch, a
sensuality that transcended mere feeling and scaled the
heights.

Emma felt as if she was slowly drowning in a deep,
translucent pool where sheer sensation ruled. Hardly
aware of what she was doing, she let her arms creep up to
clasp behind his neck as she unconsciously moved close
against him.

His mouth coaxed hers, seeking a possession she was
afraid to give, and his tongue became an erotic
instrument in subtle persuasion as one hand held her
nape, while the other slid up to cup one burgeoning
breast, teasing its swollen peak into tantalising
awareness.

It would be so easy to agree to sexual fulfilment, and
for a moment she was almost tempted. Out of curiosity, a
sheer need to discover if his sensual expertise extended to
dispensing with her frigidity. Would this pulsing ache
deep within dissipate and leave her feeling disappointed
and somehow deprived? Or would it flare and explode
into something glorious; be equally an orgasmic
attuning of the flesh as well as of the mind?

A feeling of self-loathing rose to the fore, and with it

came guilt and a sense of disloyalty. How could she think like this, let alone consider . . .

With a whimper of distress she pulled away from him, shaken by the depth of her arousal and the ease with which he was able to achieve it.

Slowly she lifted her eyes to his, glimpsing little more than a keen scrutiny in his expression.

'I shall have to plead temporary insanity,' she said at last. 'Anything else would be impossible.'

A muscle tautened along his jaw, making his features appear harsh and forbidding. 'Would it?' His wry smile was not in the least kind, and her lips pursed slightly, then began to tremble at the thought of his ability to look into her soul.

'I'm going back to bed,' she declared, wanting only to get away from him.

'What a shame you insist it must be alone.'

'Would you believe I prefer it that way?'

'No,' said Nick with dangerous softness. 'Not if the way you react to me is any indication.'

Such a damning accusation was almost her undoing, and she felt a flood of colour heat her cheeks; then they went white, almost ashen. 'I hate you,' she breathed bitterly. 'My God, you can't know how much!'

Without a further word she stepped round him and made her way upstairs to her room, uncaring whether he followed or not.

CHAPTER EIGHT

THE panoramic vista of Naples, its beautiful, picturesque bay with the Isles of Ischia and Capri at its entrance, was a scenic delight. Vineyards and citrus groves dotted the hillside on the Bay's eastern shore, and the many houses with their multi-coloured roof-tiles, dulled and aged by the years, provided a pleasant contrast.

Emma had elected to wear a light cotton skirt with a blouse in spearmint green. The shade suited her colouring and looked both cool and fresh. Nick had stipulated casual attire, and he looked incredibly fit and virile in cream cotton Levis and a matching short-sleeved shirt. Annalisa chattered virtually non-stop during the drive down, and Emma was grateful for the young girl's presence. It made it easier to project a façade of normality; temporarily to forget what had transpired the previous evening.

From Sorrento they boarded the hydrofoil out to Capri, the fabled green isle of the Parthenopean Gulf, where they stopped at the Blue Grotto. The limestone sea cave was truly spectacular, with water reflections casting an eerily beautiful iridescence, a translucence that resembled a rare silk-encased jewel.

After a late lunch, eaten at one of Sorrento's colourful restaurants, Nick headed the Ferrari along the rugged coast road. Negotiating the twisting hairpin bends of Amalfi Drive took all his concentration, and Emma was unable to dampen her acute apprehension at the dramatically steep hillsides of the magnificent ravine which plunged down to the sea.

It was impossible not to be alarmed, and seated closest to the perilous drop made it all the worse. Perhaps if she closed her eyes . . . Damn! Assuring herself that Nick was an expert driver did little to aid her rapidly shredding nerves! Positano, with its pink, white and yellow houses perched precipitously against the perpendicular hillsides, was a revelation, and masses of bougainvillaea provided a colourful splash in contrast to the wide expanse of aquamarine sea.

By the time they reached Amalfi, Emma was a quivering wreck, and she viewed Nick's suggestion to stop for refreshments with immense relief.

'Can we have pizza, *Papa*?'

'Of course, if that is what you want.' He paused at a junction, then drove until he was able to park close to a *ristorante*. 'This should do.' He turned slightly and smiled, and Emma summoned every ounce of acting ability in an effort to appear relaxed.

'Wasn't that exciting?' Annalisa demanded as she slipped out from the car. 'I loved all the olive and lemon groves and the scent of orange blossom, the steep hills and all the twists and bends in the road. Didn't you, Emma?'

How could she say no, when the scenery was exquisite? Or spoil the young girl's pleasure by explaining that since being involved in a car accident a year ago she had developed a morbid fear of travelling as a passenger in *any* vehicle, no matter how competent the driver? It was a natural fear, her doctor had assured her, that would gradually lessen with time.

'It was beautiful,' she agreed, and started visibly when Nick caught hold of her elbow.

His eyes narrowed, and she bore his intent scrutiny with equanimity. 'You have become very pale. Are you feeling unwell?'

Oh, lord, Emma deplored silently. She'd have to get a grip on herself. 'I'm fine,' she assured him steadily, summoning a faint smile as she diverted her attention to Annalisa. 'Thirsty for something long and cool. Aren't you?'

'*Yes,*' the young girl enthused with an impish grin. 'In a tall glass, and *icy*!' She looked up at her father. 'Can we sit outside, *Papa*? I think watching people is fun, don't you?'

'I can see I am outnumbered,' Nick declared with mock resignation as he led them to an unoccupied table. Then, when they were comfortably seated, he sought their opinion on which type of pizza they should order.

'Seafood, with lots of cheese, capsicum and *everything*,' his daughter announced ravenously. 'Do say you like seafood, Emma,' she went on to implore. 'We love it, don't we, *Papa*?'

Nick let his gaze rest with affection on his daughter's shining head, then shifted a gleaming glance to Emma. 'Don't be unduly influenced,' he drawled musingly. 'It is possible to order pizza in a variety of sizes. You must have what you want.'

'Seafood will be fine. It's a favourite of mine.'

'We never have pizza at school, and Teresa refuses to make it for me more than once when I am home,' Annalisa declared.

'My housekeeper,' Nick explained drolly, 'is a woman who considers her culinary talents exceed the demands of pizza.'

'That is why *Papa* indulges me during the holidays,' Annalisa enlightened, throwing her father a beauteous smile, to which he responded with a gentle brush of his fingers to her cheek.

Emma felt something tighten with pain deep within that was difficult to explain. A sense of loss; envy, perhaps, of the genuine loving and caring that father and daughter shared. They represented a complete unit that was seemingly without need of a wife and mother. Why not, when there were a string of attractive women waiting discreetly in the wings to satisfy Nick's sexual appetite, and Annalisa was adequately cared for between Silvana, boarding school and her father? Emma knew she would be sad to relinquish their friendship when she left Italy. Sharing their company had proved a welcome salve to her own wounds, yet it had succeeded in opening the deepest and most hurtful of them all; the recognition that love possessed many facets, of which Marc had commanded only one.

The startling clarity of this discovery should have caused surprise. Instead, she was filled with a sense of release, almost freedom.

'Emma? I thought you were thirsty.'

For one split second she felt completely disorientated as she dragged her mind back from the past, and she proffered an apologetic smile across the table. 'I'm sorry, I was miles away.' She included Nick by sweeping a glance in his direction, then felt her eyes widen beneath his steady gaze, aware to her considerable chagrin that he knew just where her thoughts had been centred and their ultimate conclusion.

Dear lord in heaven—was she so transparent? It wasn't fair that he possessed the ability to read her mind, when *his* was a mystery. She knew he regarded her with affection, but affection affiliated to *what*? Was she simply a pretty diversion to fill his holiday, a companion for his daughter on their numerous excursions? If that were true, why had he kissed her with such dreamy sweetness and wrought havoc to her tender emotions? She frequently swung like a pendulum between agony and ecstasy, stricken by an angry helplessness at her awakening desire, yet rendered intensely vulnerable by her own fragility where he was concerned.

A decision to confirm her return flight to Sydney strengthened her resolve to leave Rome at the soonest opportunity, otherwise she was seriously in danger of losing the tenuous hold she had on her own sanity. To stay any longer was cruel, not only to herself, but to Annalisa, for there was little doubt that the young girl had become very fond of her Australian relative.

The arrival of a waiter with their order proved a welcome distraction, and Emma picked up a wedge of deliciously aromatic pizza and bit into it with relish, laughing when she was urged by Annalisa to take another piece.

It was half an hour before they made their way back to the car, contentedly replete, and ready for the last leg of coastal road to Salerno where they would pick up the autostrada direct to Rome.

Small villages dotted the landscape, charming, and so quiet they could have belonged to a former century, Emma decided as the Ferrari purred along the smooth ribbon of winding bitumen. Some of the houses bore the evidence of time, heightened by vivid splashes of colour portrayed by flowering plants in innumerable clay pots. It was too late to see young children at play, but there were fishing vessels anchored in one of the bays and yards of netting spread wide to dry.

Perhaps it was the food, or the numerous hours of travel, but Emma felt her eyelids begin to droop as weariness descended. Annalisa had become strangely quiet, and a glance towards the rear seat ascertained the young girl had fallen asleep.

It would be wonderful to give in to the weight of somnolence, and doze. Dared she? Nick wouldn't mind, in fact, he'd probably appreciate being able to concentrate solely on driving instead of keeping up a commentary on passing points of interest.

Gently lowering her lashes, she allowed herself a masked peep at his profile, admiring the strength in repose, a relaxation she could never hope to emulate. He looked totally in control, his movements at the wheel merely an extension of the vehicle as he negotiated the road.

Emma sensed his sudden alertness an instant before the vehicle braked, then swerved sharply to the right. It happened so quickly there was no time to prepare for the sickening thud as the Ferrari lurched into a concrete post.

A variety of sounds reverberated inside her head all at once; Annalisa's shocked cry, Nick's muffled oath, the horrendous screech of car brakes.

'Emma? Annalisa? Are you hurt?'

Nick's voice penetrated her stunned brain, and she added her own assurance to that of his daughter. The impact had left her more shaken than anything, and she bore his swift, analytical scrutiny in silence before he turned to check Annalisa.

Emma was aware that he had slipped out from behind the wheel, and she heard his deep voice, clipped and chillingly quiet, amid a stream of voluble Italian. She

could see two pretty girls and two brash young men
standing beside an expensive sports car. On their way to
a party, and the driver presumably out to impress his
passengers with a burst of speed round a hairpin bend.

'I was asleep,' Annalisa professed, her eyes wide with a
mixture of shock and excitement, and Emma fought
down the feeling of nausea that threatened to engulf her
by taking several deep breaths in an effort to restore calm
to her shattered nerves. 'Are you all right, Emma? You
look white.'

She lifted a hand and ran shaky fingers through her
hair. 'I'm fine, really.' Somehow she had to dampen this
terrible sense of fear, precipitating memories of another
accident, thus providing a terrifying feeling of *déjà vu*.
Haunting and all too vivid was the crash scene in which
Marc had been killed, and for a few petrifying minutes
she was back there, reliving every painful detail in her
mind.

It seemed an age before Nick returned to the car, time
which she'd filled by recounting the day's events with
Annalisa; and gradually the enormity of what could
have been had begun to fade.

'I'll call the police, then arrange for a tow-truck,' Nick
announced as he slid behind the wheel, and reached for
the mobile telephone set into the centre console.

'Won't we be able to drive back to Rome, *Papa*?'

'Not tonight, *piccina*.' He pressed the final digit, then
spoke into the receiver as he relayed the relevant
information.

Why hadn't it occurred to her that they would be
unable to continue their journey? Emma queried
silently. Damage to the Ferrari precluded travelling so
much as one kilometre, let alone a few hundred!

With smooth efficiency Nick arranged for the car to be towed to a garage in the nearby village of Vietri Mare, then he organised accommodation, rang Rosa to inform her of their delay, and finally, what was to prove the highlight of the evening for Annalisa—a lift into Vietri Mare in the police car when all the details had been completed.

The *pensione* was small, and the suite they were given immaculately neat and clean. Situated on the second floor it comprised two bedrooms, each of which led off from a central lounge. There was a functional bathroom and facilities to make tea or coffee. Breakfast, Nick told them, would be served in their suite at eight the following morning.

'We will have to sleep in our underwear,' Annalisa declared, apparently delighted by the novelty of it all, and she burst into undisguised laughter at her father's wry smile.

'Fortunately the *signora* who runs this humble establishment prepares for any emergency. She has been able to supply an assortment of toiletries, and extra towels. I am sure we'll manage.'

Emma managed a faint smile. 'How extensive is the Ferrari's damage?'

'It requires some basic repair work to make it roadworthy.' He raked a hand through his hair. 'I'll get the panel work done once we get back to Rome.'

'Will it take long, *Papa*?'

'Much depends on whether the local Ferrari agent has the necessary parts,' Nick declared. 'If not, he will have to send to Salerno.' He effected an imperceptible shrug. 'With luck, we should be able to leave late tomorrow.'

'Otherwise we get to stay another night,' Annalisa

stated solemnly. 'We might have to buy more clothes.' An irrepressible grin appeared, and her eyes sparkled mischievously. 'I will have an adventure to tell everyone when I get back to school. What fun!'

Emma privately thought she could do without just such an adventure! What it was to have the uncomplicated vision of the young, she decided with envy. Annalisa was extremely fortunate in having a father with sufficient power and wealth at his command to ensure maximum service was accomplished in the swiftest possible time.

It was quite late, well after eleven o'clock, and she glimpsed Annalisa's stifled yawn and offered a sympathetic smile. 'It's been a long day,' she pointed out gently. 'Do you want to go to bed?'

The young girl appeared a trifle reluctant, then she relented with a rueful grin. 'I think so.' Her eyes brightened considerably. 'You will share with me, won't you, Emma?' She looked askance at her father. 'You don't mind, do you, *Papa*?'

'Not unless Emma would prefer a room to herself,' Nick stipulated, and Emma felt her heart lurch, then begin a rapid beat as his gaze rested overlong on her slightly flustered features.

There was faint mockery evident in those dark depths that upset her composure and did strange things to her breathing. With considerable effort she dragged her eyes away from his and turned towards Annalisa. 'I don't mind sharing with you,' she said quietly. 'I'm feeling tired, too. Shall we both say goodnight to your father now?'

'Yes. We can talk for a while, can't we? Like sisters do,' the young girl declared happily, and reaching out she caught hold of Emma's hand, then she stretched up and planted a generous kiss to her father's cheek.

'Goodnight, *piccina*. Sleep well,' Nick bade, lifting his head.

'Do you want to kiss Emma, too, *Papa*?'

Innocence, or calculated guile? Emma pondered in a haze of embarrassment as she deliberately kept her eyes fixed on the hollow at the base of his throat, and she prayed fervently he would dismiss bestowing such a gesture.

'Why not?'

She heard his smooth query, then she stood completely still as he leant forward and kissed her softly parted mouth with considerable thoroughness.

'Goodnight, Emma.'

It took every ounce of will-power to retain a hold on her temper. How dared he subject her to such a display in front of Annalisa? Expose her to something that could so easily be misconstrued?

Emma didn't deign to look at him, and without a further word she turned and made her way with Annalisa to the bedroom they had elected to occupy for the night.

'Are you cross with me because I asked *Papa* to kiss you?' the young girl queried hesitantly as soon as the door closed behind them.

Emma was about to say *yes*, when she caught sight of the wretched uncertainty mirrored in Annalisa's expression, and she softened her rebuke with a slight smile. 'Not really.' With your father, she added silently, for taking unfair advantage of the situation.

'You do like him, don't you?'

What could she say? *Any* answer at all was potentially dangerous.

'I've enjoyed sharing his company with you,' she said carefully.

'Do you think you would like to—live in Italy?'

Oh lord, this was getting worse by the minute! She could see the wistful hope in Annalisa's hazel eyes, a fervent, childish wish to play matchmaker to two adults, one of whom she adored and wanted more than anything to provide her with a mother.

'My home is in Australia,' she answered gently. 'I have parents who would miss me dreadfully if I moved away.'

Annalisa was silent for several minutes, then her eyes misted with unshed tears. 'You think I am being silly, don't you?'

'Sweetheart, *no*! Never silly,' she answered swiftly, and she gathered the young girl's slight figure close against her own, feeling her throat constrict as small arms curled round her waist.

'I like you so much,' Annalisa vowed with muffled fervour. 'I wish you could stay for ever.'

'My boss would give me the sack,' Emma joked in an attempt at lightness. 'Then what would I do?'

'*Papa* could find you a job. I know he could.'

She felt the faint tremor that shook Annalisa's body, and she cursed Nick afresh for being instrument in fostering a young child's romantic dreams.

'We've had a lovely time together, haven't we?' she queried gently.

'Just like a real family.'

'We all indulge in pretend games, Annalisa,' she began quietly, stroking the silky hair with soothing movements. 'Even adults. Sadly, it isn't always possible to change make-believe into reality.'

'But I want it so badly.'

'I'm sure your father does everything he can to see that you are well cared for and content.' She took hold of Annalisa's chin and lifted it a little. 'Would you want him to be unhappy? He must have loved your mother very much—perhaps too much to think of allowing anyone to take her place.'

'I never knew her,' Annalisa owned wretchedly, and Emma's heart tightened painfully, feeling the young girl's hurt as if it were her own.

'The photographs you showed me of her were lovely. She was very beautiful.' A lump rose up in her throat as the celluloid vision of a laughing attractive young woman sprang readily to mind. Anna Castelli had held the world in her hands by virtue of being Nick Castelli's wife. Her eyes had glowed with it, and Emma experienced a shaft of pure, unadulterated jealousy slice through to her very soul. 'Just as you will be in a few short years,' she added unsteadily.

'Do you think so?' Annalisa queried doubtfully. 'Do I really look like my mother?'

'Really,' Emma declared softly. 'Now, shall we undress and get into bed? You use the bathroom first, while I turn down the covers, then I'll have a shower.'

Within minutes of slipping between the sheets Annalisa was asleep, her measured breathing indicative of a swift passage into blissful slumber. Not so Emma, who found it increasingly impossible to fall asleep. Even counting sheep didn't help, nor did any one of several relaxing techniques. In the end she simply gave up and resigned herself to laying awake until sheer weariness provided its own release.

Somehow she must have dozed without being aware of it, for she came sharply awake, still in the grip of a fearful nightmare, where it was dark and damp and the sound of her own screams mingled with those of several wailing sirens. She was in the car, and she was hurting, and there was a male body slumped grotesquely over the wheel beside her.

It was so vivid, so *real*, she could smell the spilt petrol, hear the voices of the men who dragged her clear, then the terrifying *whoosh* as the car ignited into flames.

God, oh dear God, *no*! Silent tears trickled down her cheeks unchecked as she stared sightlessly into the darkness.

It's all right, a tiny voice soothed, *it's all right*, it's just a bad dream. It's over, you're here, safe and alive. Just breathe deeply. But Marc is dead, she longed to scream.

Except she didn't, and gradually reality overtook the insanity of re-lived memory.

With shaking movements she brushed the wetness from her face, then she lay still, recalling all the pleasant events in her life with cold-hearted determination.

CHAPTER NINE

AN hour later Emma was still staring at the ceiling, and the faint niggle at each temple had become a throbbing headache. A silent curse whispered in the darkness of the room. Now there was no hope of sleep, only the promise of enervating pain unless she took something to alleviate it. There were some tablets in her bag, and gingerly she slid out of bed and quietly wound one of the huge bathtowels sarong-wise round her body.

Sleeping *au naturel* wasn't something she normally indulged in, but there was little choice if she wanted to don fresh underwear in the morning. The light, wispy nylon would dry in a few hours, spread over a towel in her room, and she felt their slight dampness now, then shook her head. What did it matter? She was adequately covered, and besides, Nick was behind a closed door on the opposite side of the lounge. It would take only a few minutes to get some water from the bathroom and wash down two tablets.

Extracting the strip of foil from her bag, she quietly made her way from the room and crossed the lounge to the bathroom. Once there she switched on the light, then turned the faucet and half filled a glass with water.

She had just replaced it on the pedestal beside the white porcelain basin when she felt the hairs prickle at the back of her neck, and she moved her head in seemingly slow motion, half fearful whether some sixth sense had alerted her to the presence of another human or whether it was a figment of her imagination.

The last person she expected to see was Nick. No, she corrected dazedly—he was the last person she'd hoped to see.

'Unable to sleep?'

His voice was quiet, and she blinked, finding it difficult to focus on his features, for razing pain had seeped behind her eyes.

'I'm sorry if I disturbed you.' Her hand fluttered to the tucked edge of her towel, supremely conscious of her attire.

He moved further forward into the light, and she saw he too wore a towel, although his was knotted carelessly at his waist and reached his knees. The result was an expanse of muscular chest whorled with dark hair, broad shoulders, and an overall portrayal of silent, deadly strength.

'I was still awake.' He gave an imperceptible shrug as he shortened the distance between them. 'What is it? A headache?'

'Yes.' Her monosyllabic answer was scarcely more than a whisper, and she glimpsed his slight frown, the faint narrowing of his eyes, then her chin was taken between firm fingers and lifted so that she had little option but to bear his scrutiny.

'Where?' He gently probed one temple, then the other. 'There?'

'Yes,' she whispered, incapable of uttering another word, and of their own volition each eyelid drifted down in unison, hiding the pain and anguish from his view.

'What did you take? Prescribed medication?'

The action of his fingers was incredibly soothing, a tactile massage she could have borne indefinitely.

'Emma?'

She wanted to lay her head into the curve of his shoulder and absorb his strength, pretend for a short space of time that she was infinitely precious and possessed the right to expect his comfort.

'*Cara*——'

It was the endearment that did it, the careless affectionate inflection in his voice. Her eyes pricked with hot hears, then welled and spilled to trickle in slow twin rivulets down to her chin.

'Sweet Mother of God,' he muttered huskily. 'I was desperately afraid tonight's accident might revive that ill-fated crash.'

She didn't care any more, she just wanted solace to expiate a haunting memory, and she offered no resistance as he drew her into his arms.

It was like coming home: to warmth, security, and something much, much more. She could feel the faint stir of his breath against her hair, the steady thud of his heartbeat beneath her cheek.

With a featherlight touch Nick brushed his lips across one exposed temple, then trailed down to the sensitive cord at the edge of her neck. He created a slow, leisurely path along a pulsing hollow, caressing it with his tongue, teasing the delicate pulse that began to quicken beneath his touch, urging the beat to a thudding crescendo before lifting her head so that he could possess her mouth.

Slowly, with incredible sensitivity, he sought a response she was desperately afraid to give. There was a wealth of seduction in his touch that was impossible to ignore, and she gave a silent gasp as he caught hold of her lower lip between his teeth, nibbling at the full curve as he traced its outline with the tip of his tongue.

It was hopelessly erotic, transcending mere pleasure, and she moved restlessly in his arms, unconsciously wanting more.

A slow ache began in the region of her stomach, spreading in an ever-increasing circle, until her entire body seemed to radiate with passionate desire.

Emma closed her eyes, drowning in sheer sensation as his lips moved down to the edge of her towel, which somehow no longer provided any restriction. She cried out as his mouth took possession of one roseate peak, rolling it gently with his tongue before catching it between his teeth and applying sufficient pressure to place her on a knife-edge between intense pleasure and the threat of pain.

Somehow she seemed to be floating, transported high on to a sensual plateau from which she never wanted to descend, and it wasn't until she felt the soft cotton sheets beneath her back that she realised they were no longer in the lounge.

A subtle glow from a dimmed bedside lamp provided the room's only illumination, and was sufficient for her to be aware that she no longer wore the towel. Nor did Nick, his splendid, tautly muscled body a potent force, and her eyes dilated with a mixture of shock, anguish and pain, then became luminous as she silently begged fulfilment—too caught up with an aching physical need to struggle with her conscience.

Afterwards she would fight self-inflicted recriminations, undoubtedly hate herself for not rising up out of this illusory torpor which appeared responsible for weighting her limbs and keeping her enmeshed within a sensual web so powerful that only total satiation could provide its release.

Nick's mouth closed over hers, caressing, teasing, promising; yet just as she thought he'd deepen the kiss, his lips softened to brush a tantalising, evocative path over the curve of her mouth, until with a groan she lifted her hands and encircled his neck, tangling her fingers in the thick hair at his nape to hold fast his head.

Her body moved against his, unconsciously inviting his possession. Deliberately releasing her arms, he began a shameless exploration of the soft hollows at the base of her throat before moving lower to savour the delicate curves of one breast with its sensitised, hardened peak, then traced a path to its twin.

Slowly, with sensuous ease, his lips edged down over her ribcage, seeking the soft indentation of her navel before trailing lower.

Her shocked protest brought no respite, and she was powerless to still the restless movements of her limbs as they threshed impotently against the promised ecstasy of his touch; wanting, craving for him to continue, yet too caught up with untutored inhibitions to allow him licence to what he sought.

His mouth lifted to graze across her hip before tracing a path over her stomach to caress the curve of her waist, moving higher until his lips claimed hers in a deep, drugging kiss that wiped out any uncertainty.

A treacherous hunger clamoured assuagement, and soft whimpering sounds emerged from her throat as she begged his possession, crying out as his head lowered once more to discover her ultimate feminine core.

With deliberate eroticism he introduced her to an experience so fraught with sensual ecstasy she was unable to control its tide as it washed through her body, each successive wave seeming to lift her higher on to yet another sensory plateau.

Just as she thought she'd scaled the heights, he began to feather light kisses in a steady upward trail to her breasts, and her body arched of its own volition as he bestowed each a lingering caress, then leapt with hunger as he lowered his body over hers and effected one sure thrust.

She cried out as he began a slow, gentle pacing, withholding his pleasure until her body was in perfect accord with his own, then he guided her toward a euphoric vortex of emotion.

Afterwards she lay spent, consumed with a sweet lethargy that made the simplest movement an effort. Even *thinking* about what had transpired between them brought a resurgence of languorous warmth, and her eyes flew wide open as Nick trailed gentle fingers across her cheek, then smoothed the thick auburn curls from her temple.

Don't say anything, she implored silently. Don't spoil something so beautiful, I'll probably never again know its equal.

His lips moved to her shoulder, caressing the delicate curves and hollows, before wandering with tactile sensuality to tease the lobe of her ear, taking it between his teeth then releasing it as he lifted a hand to her chin and forced her to meet his gaze.

Emma let her lashes sweep down, protectively veiling her eyes, knowing the deep, slumbrous passion evident in their depths would reveal with startling clarity the extent of her emotions.

She could feel his breath warm on her face as he leant forward and covered her lips with his own, softly, with a tenderness that made her want to cry. Then she gave an incredulous gasp as he caught hold of her hand and gently slid off Marc's wedding band and slipped it on to the third finger of her right hand.

Without a word he lifted her left hand to his lips, brushing them against the pale, exposed strip of skin, and her eyes dilated with dawning anguish.

Remorse, shame, flowed through her body, all-consuming as it mingled with guilt and a number of other equally untenable feelings.

'Let go of the past, *cara*.'

'I can't.' It was a cry from the heart, and she strove hard to regain her composure, hating herself, and *Nick*, with an intensity that was frightening.

'You can,' he insisted quietly, and her breathing became ragged as her eyes filled with distress.

'You're asking too much!' Emma whispered emotionally, wrenching against the hands that held her as she fought to be free. Except Nick wouldn't let her go, and she began to struggle in earnest, hating the ease with which he was able to reduce her wildly threshing form to impotent helplessness.

His arms were like bands of steel, moulding her against his body as if he intended for her to absorb some of his strength, and after a while she became less rigid, her agitation decreasing as her breathing began to quieten.

Slowly, with gradual perceptiveness, she became aware of the soothing movement of his hand as he traced a gentle path down the length of her spine, across her shoulders, then slid to her nape as his fingers began a tactile massage of the tense cores at the base of her scalp.

His head moved slightly, and she felt his lips brush her forehead, then rest against one throbbing temple, caressing it with sensitivity for what seemed an age.

With infinite gentleness he trailed his lips down to the

edge of her jaw, then slipped lower to the delicate hollows at the base of her neck, tasting the sweet indentations with unhurried ease.

'Please,' she begged brokenly as a traitorous warmth began to unfurl itself and steal treacherously through her veins. She felt herself tremble, and tears welled up behind her eyes until they became large pools of shimmering gold. 'Don't. I couldn't bear it.'

His lips grazed the length of her throat, and she felt, sensed, his murmured endearment as they settled on the edge of her mouth to tease the fullness of her lower lip before beginning a gentle probing exploration of the soft moistness within.

Nothing seemed to matter except the hungry desire spiralling through her body, encompassing and all-consuming until she became a willing supplicant, *his* to command in any way he chose.

'Stay with me.' His voice was deep and husky, his gaze gleaming with passionate intensity, yet there was a stillness about him, almost as if he was waiting for her willing complicance.

Comprehension brought forth a gamut of emotions, and she dared not look at him, or she'd be swept away by a complexity of sensations too diverse to analyse.

'No,' she refused with a strangled gasp, and her eyes dilated with sheer torment as she stammered quickly, 'What you're asking—isn't fair. Annalisa——' Her voice trailed off, then returned in agonised indecision. 'How can I?' She was almost shaking with reaction, becoming aware of her nakedness, his. She looked wildly for something to cover herself, and grabbed hold of a nearby towel and wound it sarong-wise round her body. 'Please,' she implored, 'don't you see that it isn't possible?'

His gaze was carefully inscrutable, his fingers gentle as they brushed lightly across her cheek. 'I can't persuade you to change your mind?'

All too easily, she declared silently as she shook her head in mute negation. 'I must go.' It became imperative to leave now, if she was to retain a shred of sanity, and she almost ran towards the door in her hurry to get away.

'Emma.'

There was something in his voice that brought her to a standstill, and she let go of the doorknob and slowly turned back to face him.

'Thank you,' he said gently.

How could she respond to that? Reciprocate and assure him he was the most sensitive man she'd ever had the pleasure to know? Her limited experience with men precluded the necessary *savoir-faire* to utter even a simple acknowledgment, and she dragged her eyes away from the paganistic splendour he represented and moved quickly from the room.

In the bathroom she quietly closed the door behind her and stepped beneath the shower, then she soaped every square inch of skin until it glowed before she rinsed off the suds and emerged to towel herself dry.

A quick glance in the mirror drew forth a startled gasp, and her eyes widened in disbelief that the reflected mirror-image was herself. Why, she looked positively *ethereal*! Her mouth was soft and slightly swollen, and her eyes ... They bore a dreamy expression, their depths secretive and gleaming with the intense satisfaction of sexual satiation. Anyone seeing her now would be in no doubt as to how she'd spent the previous few hours. All the evidence was there, and she closed her eyes in self-remorse, fearful that life would never again be the same.

Don't think, she bade herself silently as she wound the towel around her slim curves and switched off the light.

Within seconds she slid between the sheets of the bed in the room she shared with Annalisa, and she endeavoured to cull sleep in the hope it would provide a blissful oblivion from the numerous condemnations invading her brain.

Perhaps a guardian angel looked down with beneficence, for it seemed only minutes before her eyelids fluttered closed, and she woke to the sound of Annalisa's bright voice mingling with that of Nick's deeper tones just outside the bedroom door.

'Shall we wake Emma, do you think, *Papa*? Breakfast is ready, and it will get cold.'

'Just a little longer, *piccina*, hmm? We can always order more later.'

Without thought Emma threw back the covers and slid to her feet. Gathering up her clothes, she quickly donned bra and panties, then stepped into her half-slip and pulled on her skirt and blouse. Her hair, she groaned silently. What on earth could she do to restore it to some kind of order? The small brush she carried in her bag was totally inadequate for anything more than the briefest tidying of her tumbled tresses. At least the village shops would open this morning and she could buy the necessary requisites!

With a nervous gesture she smoothed the belt at her waist and fingered the top button on her blouse, then she took a deep breath and crossed to the door.

'Good morning.' The words sounded overbright and false, even to her own ears and, while she offered Annalisa a warm smile, she let her gaze skim towards Nick without meeting his eyes. She couldn't. After last night, it took all her courage to face him.

'Emma, you were fast asleep when I woke!' Annalisa cried as she closed the space between them. 'Come and eat breakfast. There's cereal and fruit, toast, coffee. Or you can have eggs, with *prosciutto* or salami.'

'Toast and coffee will be fine,' she said quickly, and privately thought she'd be fortunate if she ate anything at all.

'I trust you slept well?' Nick queried, and Emma aimed a quick smile in the direction of his right shoulder.

'Yes, thank you,' she responded evenly. He knew precisely how she'd spent a few hours of the night, none of which had been occupied with *sleeping*!

'Shall I pour you some coffee, Emma?' Annalisa asked solicitously, wielding the silver pot with ease as she filled her father's cup.

'Please. I'd love some.'

It was like playing a game, Emma determined with detachment. Nick's smile was as warm and friendly as it had ever been, his manner that of a man relaxed and totally at ease. Beneath the fringe of her lowered lashes she had the opportunity to view him unobserved—or so she thought until she incurred a gleaming glance full of passionate intensity, and something else she was unwilling to define.

Thank heavens for Annalisa's presence, otherwise she wouldn't be sitting across the table sharing something as mundane as breakfast. The promise of precisely *where* she would be was reflected momentarily in his eyes, and a shaft of exquisite pleasure rose from deep within, spiralling rapidly until it encompassed her entire body.

It was maddening to feel so—*possessed*, she decided shakily, aware that her breathing had quickened considerably and there was a painful lump in her throat.

Consequently it was a relief to escape the confines of their suite and wander through the village. The Ferrari looked sadly the worse for its encounter with a post, and Nick was able to find out that the car would be ready early that evening.

For the remainder of the morning they browsed among the village shops, lunched at a seaside *bistro*, then returned to the *pensione* to observe siesta and escape the heat.

After a shower and a light meal Nick left to collect the car, and it was almost seven when they reached Salerno and joined the *autostrada* leading back to Rome.

It was late when Nick brought the car to a halt outside the villa. Annalisa had lapsed into a fitful doze during the latter part of the drive, and Emma, ever conscious of Nick's immediate presence, took the easy way out and simply closed her eyes and leaned her head back against the cushioned head-rest. It precluded the need for conversation, and quite frankly she couldn't think of a thing to say to him. Her own thoughts were damning, her sense of self-recrimination increasing with every passing hour until her mind seemed filled with jagged sequences that taunted with kaleidoscopic confusion.

'We have to talk.'

Emma lifted her head slowly and turned towards the owner of that deep, slightly accented voice.

'Whatever for?' she managed calmly, and glimpsed the slight hardening of his expression in the reflection of light illuminating the sheltered portico.

'Don't freeze me out, Emma,' Nick warned quietly, and she bit back a swift retort as Annalisa stirred into wakefulness and asked if they'd arrived home.

'Yes, we have,' her father imparted, shooting Emma a wry glance before shifting his attention to his daughter. 'And here is Zia Rosa to welcome us.'

Emma reached for the door-handle and slipped out from the car, whereupon she was immediately enveloped in an affectionate embrace, and there was very little need for her to say anything at all in light of Annalisa's excited recounting and Nick's affirmation of the facts.

'Maria will bring some refreshments,' Rosa insisted as she urged them towards the *salone*. 'You must be hungry.'

'I'm thirsty,' Annalisa pronounced. '*Papa* drove straight through without stopping.'

'After feeding you an early dinner,' Nick pointed out teasingly, and she burst into delicious laughter.

'Marinaded baby octupus! Emma was not impressed.'

'There were other selections on the menu,' he chided good-naturedly as he greeted Enzo and accepted a glass of white wine.

'Emma? What will you have?'

Wine would undoubtedly go to her head, and she needed clarity of mind if she was to bear Nick's presence with any equanimity. 'Soda water will be fine,' she acquiesced, and met Enzo's faintly raised eyebrow with a slight smile. If only she could escape to her room, yet to do so too soon would be tantamount to an admission of sorts. It was bad enough that Nick could see through her pretence. To allow Rosa and Enzo to discern any subtle change in her relationship with their nephew would be more than she could bear.

So she stayed where she was, listening as Rosa relayed a message for Nick that had come through from his office in Milan late the previous afternoon, then contained a mixture of disappointment and swift calculation when he returned from making the call to announce that he would have to absent himself for a few days.

'It cannot wait, unfortunately. An important associate has arrived unexpectedly from France, and he refuses to deal with anyone else.' One eyebrow rose in a semblance of wry resignation. 'No amount of appeasement will satisfy, despite the fact there are two men on hand more than capable of coping with him.' He shot Rosa a conciliatory smile. 'I've booked an early-morning flight. I hope you don't mind?'

'Of course not,' Rosa determined at once. 'Annalisa must stay with us.' She lifted a hand as Nick would have intervened. 'No, I insist. You have been so kind to Emma while she has been here. Now it is my turn. Together with Annalisa, we will explore the boutiques. Something, I have learned,' she continued with a wicked twinkle, 'men prefer to avoid.'

'I could easily contact Silvana and have her take care of Annalisa for the time I will be away.'

'Oh no, *Papa*,' his daughter implored. 'I would much prefer to stay here at the villa with Zia Rosa and Emma. It will be such fun, I will hardly have time to miss you.'

Nick's teeth showed white as he bit back his laughter, but his eyes were sober as he directed Emma a piercing glance, taunting silently if *she* would miss him.

She caught his crystalline gaze and a faint line of colour ran fleetingly along her cheekbones, betraying the strength of her emotions. She felt bewitched and tormented by a memory that would live with her for ever—solitary, beautiful, and never to be repeated. Tomorrow she would ring the airport and book the first plane bound for Sydney.

'It's late, *piccina*,' Nick directed gently. 'More than time you went upstairs to bed, hmm?'

The young girl looked at him earnestly. 'Will you be gone before I wake in the morning?'

'Probably,' he concurred musingly. 'I must leave the villa before six.'

'Then I'll say goodbye now.' She crossed to where he sat and twined her arms around his neck. 'Take care, *Papa*. Hurry back.'

'Indeed I shall,' he assured her, returning her kiss.

It seemed a good opportunity for Emma to make good her escape, and she rose to her feet, indicating her intention to retire.

'I'll come with you,' Nick declared, unwinding his lengthy frame from the chair. 'It's been a long day, and I have to make an early start.'

She suffered his light clasp at her elbow, only because it was impossible to wrench away. He must have sensed her disquiet, for his fingers tightened with iron-like intensity, and she stood helplessly still as Annalisa bade them goodnight and ran lightly ahead up the stairs.

'Would you prefer your bedroom, or mine?' Nick asked quietly, and silently mocked her as she broke into soft-voiced fury.

'Neither!'

'Such vehemence,' he said gently. 'When only last night you——'

'Last night was a mistake!' she cried wretchedly.

'I refuse to believe you mean that.'

Oh lord, she was falling deeper into the mire with every word she uttered! 'I'd like to go to bed,' she insisted, meeting his gaze with effort, and his eyes darkened fractionally, then lightened as they assumed a musing gleam.

'No moonlight stroll through the garden?'

'I really am tired.' Perhaps she sounded weary, for he led her upstairs to her room and before she could protest he followed her inside.

'Nick—don't. *Please*.' If he touched her, she'd break into a thousand pieces.

'Poor little girl, you sound terribly fragile in mind and spirit. Perhaps I will let you escape, after all—until I get back from Milan.' He lifted a hand and smoothed gentle fingers along the length of her jaw. 'Goodnight, *cara*.'

She closed her eyes as he brushed his lips lightly across her own, and she could have wept from the need to reach up and kiss him back.

'I'll ring tomorrow evening, about ten,' he said huskily, then he turned and left the room without so much as a backward glance.

CHAPTER TEN

'EMMA! *Darling*—over here.'

Through a sea of faces Emma caught sight of her parents and within seconds she was embraced and hugged, laughingly, lovingly besieged by countless questions. Her father took charge of her luggage, hefting the suitcases with ease, and together they made their way out to the airport car park.

It was cool, the skies bleak and heavy with imminent rain, and Emma shivered. After experiencing several weeks of Northern hemispheric sunshine, Sydney's winter temperatures seemed positively icy.

'You look so well,' Mrs Templeton enthused, her face wreathed with warm affection. 'And your tan! I'm dying to hear all about your trip.' She tucked her arm through that of her daughter's and gave it a firm squeeze. 'Postcards and letters are fine, but nothing compares with first-hand news.'

Amazing, Emma decided ruefully, that they failed to detect the misery through her outwardly cheerful façade. Inside she was breaking into a hundred tiny pieces, glad yet sad to be back home, although her emotions were in such a state of turmoil she seemed to be functioning by some form of automatic remote control.

Leaving Italy had involved subtle subterfuge, and saying goodbye to Rosa and Enzo had been the hardest part of all, not to mention Annalisa of whom she had become inordinately fond. However, there was no power on earth that could have persuaded her to stay and await Nick's return from Milan—two, three days hence.

A tiny bubble of hysterical laughter rose in her throat. They never had got around to talking. Even thinking about those fateful hours in his room brought pulsing heat vibrating through her veins until her whole body seemed to throb, aching even now with a damnable craving for his possession. It was sickening, and she didn't know who to hate more—Nick, or her own traitorous flesh.

'Two suitcases, when you left with only one. Did the airline charge you excess baggage?'

Emma forced her attention back to the present at the sound of her father's voice, and she even managed a light laugh as she slid into the rear seat of her parents' Daimler. 'I smiled sweetly,' she ventured with a deprecatory smile. 'And they let me through. Who could resist a shopping spree in Rome?'

'We'll have a lovely day together tomorrow sorting it all out,' her mother declared with all the contented happiness of a clucky hen having gathered its solitary chick beneath her protective wing.

'I thought I might go in to work,' Emma broached tentatively, and received an immediate remonstrative response.

'So soon? Surely you could leave it until Monday?'

She could, very easily. Except the thought of remaining idle at home for more than a few days was impossible. If she wanted to retain a shred of sanity, she needed to immerse herself in work.

'Just for a few hours,' she declared, compromising in

part. 'To drop off my sketches, so that Roberto can sort through them over the weekend.'

A month from now her holiday would be a pleasant memory and she would be able to relegate her encounter with Nick Castelli to its rightful place—that of a transitory romance which had no lasting importance in her life.

Except it didn't work that way. Instead of getting better with each passing day, it only became worse. She ate barely at all, and slept even less. Nick's forceful image was a vivid, haunting entity, ever present, filling her thoughts to such an extent that dispelling it became an impossibility. He was *there*, his deeply etched features imprinted in her mind, taunting and infinitely disturbing. The days were bad enough, but the nights were totally unbearable. Remembering her wanton response, the way she had actively craved his possession made her want to die with remorse and shame. Nick's musing observation that she was seemingly untouched by the heights and depths of passionate intensity was true, for Marc's lovemaking had never explored the realms of tactile sensuality to such an extent that she'd become utterly mindless, incapable of rational thought in an attempt to please as she was being pleasured, permitting liberties her untutored flesh hadn't known existed.

Flinging herself into a social whirl with numerous friends did no good at all, except to remove her presence from the house and the increasingly concerned eye of her parents.

Two weeks—no word, no letter, not even a phone call.

What did you expect? Emma demanded with unaccustomed scepticism. Nothing—*nothing*.

The words seemed to echo and re-echo in open mockery, and with a gesture of impotent despair she crossed to the dressing-table and began applying make-up in an effort to add some colour to her pale features. Attending church each Sunday with her parents was a lifelong habit, and she viewed her mirrored reflection with something akin to critical cynicism, seeing the faint—almost bruising—smudges beneath her eyes, the lack of sparkling warmth in their depths whenever she smiled. Anyone with a modicum of perception must see there was something wrong, and a derisive grimace momentarily clouded her features.

When would this agonising longing diminish and become less than an unbearable, aching need?

Lust, she dismissed hollowly. It couldn't be anything else—*could it*? Oh, dear lord, *no*—not *love*! It wasn't possible to love two men. Yet the degree of passion, the sheer magical ecstasy Nick had been able to evoke went beyond mere desire.

Shock stilled her fingers, and she gazed sightlessly ahead, riveted by her own revelation. Like a jigsaw, all the pieces began to fall slowly into place.

Nick's forceful features came to mind with startling clarity, and she closed her eyes against an awakening knowledge. Up until now she hadn't been willing to define her emotions, much less accept that love might be any part of them.

Unconsciously she sought Marc's wedding band where it still rested on the third finger of her right hand, letting her eyes sweep to the framed photograph placed within touching distance, depicting the features of a laughing young man captured on celluloid.

Of its own volition her hand reached out and she slowly traced the familiar face with a gentle finger. A pair of gleaming eyes looked back at her, so alive; his hair bore a gloss, an illusion of photographic artistry, and his mouth was parted in a carefree smile.

It was strange, she discovered with a sense of wonder, but looking at his image no longer brought the onset of pain. Just sweet regret for the loss of a very dear friend.

Almost silently she opened a drawer and withdrew a large photograph album, then she crossed to sit on the bed, opened the embossed cover, and began to leaf through the pages slowly, aware of so many memories, such a wealth of happiness, affection; love in its gentlest form, sharing, caring that encompassed every facet of their togetherness.

It seemed an age before she reached the final page, then she stood to her feet and replaced the album back into the drawer where it belonged. Somehow the action seemed symbolic with the closing of a chapter in her life.

'Emma?'

The sound of her mother's voice intruded, and she turned, summoning a smile.

'We'll be late, darling. It's almost eleven, now,' Mrs Templeton advised with a faintly anxious frown.

'I'm ready,' Emma assured as she caught up her coat from the bed and shrugged it on before collecting her shoulder-bag.

It was after midday when they arrived home, and once indoors Emma changed into designer jeans and a loose-fitting multi-coloured knitted jumper, then she made her way towards the kitchen to help prepare lunch.

Just as she was placing a casserole into the microwave

the doorbell pealed, its melodic chimes sounding inordinately loud.

'I'll get it,' Emma called, aware that her father was comfortably ensconced in the library studying the Sunday papers and her mother was in the midst of setting the table.

Who could be visiting at this hour? And on a cold day with rain lashing the house in noisy gusts that rattled the windowpanes and shook the roof struts? Two hours previously it had been fine, a false preliminary to southern hemispheric spring, sharp and cool with wind whipping through the tree branches and buffeting all that stood in its path.

Emma reached the front door and opened it, a ready smile poised in greeting, then she froze, shocked into immobility as she recognised the man standing on the sheltered porch.

Nick stood comfortably at ease, his tall frame filling the aperture, and her heart gave a sickening lurch.

Leashed strength was apparent in his stance, an almost animalistic sense of power, and his dark brown eyes bore an expression of deliberate inscrutability as they met hers, forcing her to hold his gaze before subjecting her to a swift, analytical appraisal.

'Emma.' The faintly inflected drawl held wary cynicism, and a dozen questions rushed to the fore, demanding answer, but only two rose to the surface.

What are you doing here? Why have you come? Except neither found voice, and she wondered hysterically if she was in the grip of some nerve-racking form of paralysis.

'Aren't you going to ask me in?'

No! The emphatic denial screamed in immediate

response, and for a few horrifying seconds she thought the sound had actually escaped her throat. Raw, aching pain clenched in her stomach, and for one heart-stopping second she considered shutting the door in his face, sure that his image was nothing more than a cruel quirk of her own damnable imagination.

Confusion reigned as a multitude of conflicting thoughts raced without coherence through her brain, and she knew with chilling certainty that there could be no escape.

It was there in his eyes, a seemingly calm inflexibility combined with indomitable will—almost as if he was issuing a silent threat.

'Who is it, darling?'

Oh lord, her mother, half-way down the hall, and certainly within hearing distance.

'Emma?' Mrs Templeton came to a faltering halt within touching distance, her pleasant features schooled into polite enquiry as they caught sight of the tall, casual but elegantly dressed man standing in her doorway. 'Is something wrong?'

With skilled adroitness Nick introduced himself, explained both his recent arrival and his connection with the Martinero family, by which time Mrs Templeton had ushered him inside and divested him of his coat, while Emma stood unable to utter so much as a word, hearing with sickening clarity the invitation her mother extended him to join them for lunch.

The next few minutes held all the connotations of a comic farce as her father was summoned from the library, and somehow Emma found herself seated in the lounge with a drink in her hand.

'Do sit down, my dear fellow,' Mr Templeton insisted heartily. 'Let me get you something to drink. Wine? Or would you prefer something stronger?'

Emma took an appreciative sip of wine from the goblet, glad of an excuse to occupy her hands as Nick accepted whisky and soda and then lowered his length into a chair directly opposite her own.

Attired in dark hip-hugging trousers, an equally dark shirt beneath a black V-necked jumper, he looked vaguely satanical and as much of a threat to her equilibrium as he had been within the first week of her meeting him.

The need to say something forced a polite query from her lips. 'When did you arrive?'

His eyes held hers with unwavering scrutiny, and the seconds seemed interminably long before he informed her, with damning imperturbability, 'Yesterday.'

Yesterday? He'd been here for more than twenty-four hours, and she hadn't known? Surely some instinctive defence mechanism should have warned her? Yesterday she'd calmly driven into the city, put in two extra hours at work assembling co-ordinates for an important client, eaten, slept, all the while ignorant and unaware that he was *here*? It didn't seem possible.

'I presume you've come on business?'

His gaze was bleak, dark with an indefinable quality she was unable to penetrate. 'No.'

Emma's heart gave a jolt, then began to thud loudly against her ribs. The sound seemed to reach her ears, momentarily filling them, and she was conscious of the rapid pulse-beat at the base of her throat—so much so, that she lifted a defensive hand to shield it from view.

'How long are you staying?' Was that her voice? So polite, *calm*, when inside she was a mass of conflicting emotions.

'As long as it takes.'

To do what? she longed to scream.

After what seemed an age, Mrs Templeton announced lunch was ready, and seated across the table from him Emma attempted to do some justice to the excellent casserole.

Nick, damn him, ate with evident enjoyment, and gave every indication of being totally at ease. Emma's parents, while seemingly benevolent hosts, couldn't help but be aware of the electric tension generated between their daughter and their guest, and were doubtless curious as to the reason why.

To say her parents were intrigued by Nick Castelli's presence was an understatement, and all through lunch Emma could sense their veiled evaluation of him.

His visit here *now* was the antithesis of coincidence, and her mind seethed with a multitude of possibilities—none of which provided a satisfactory answer.

All her senses seemed to have developed a heightened awareness, and she was acutely concious of him, the muscular tautness of his countenance, the breadth of his shoulders. It was crazy, but she wanted to reach out and touch him, feel the strength of him beneath her hands, his mouth on hers as he transported her high on to an illusory, elusive plateau where sheer sensation surpassed all rational thought.

The knowledge lent a haunting quality to her finely moulded features, a faint breathlessness to her voice as the meal progressed, and it irked her unbearably that he knew. Not only *knew*, but he seemed to be silently taunting her with her own perceptiveness.

'Could you spare Emma for a few hours?' he enquired with studied indolence, daring her to refuse as he added quietly, 'Sightseeing is infinitely more pleasurable in the company of someone familiar with this beautiful city.'

'Of course Emma must go with you,' Mrs Templeton declared at once. 'Rosa and Enzo mentioned how kind you were to Emma when she stayed with them in Rome. It's the very least she can do in return.'

Oh, he was far too shrewd for his own good, Emma seethed in frustrated silence. Couldn't her parents see that he had deliberately contrived to get her alone?

'Fetch your coat, darling. It will be cold outside,' her mother bade, unaware that Emma was already cold, shivering with an unspecified fear that had as its base the agony of Nick's unknown intention once they left the sanctuary of her home.

One thing was remarkably clear, she decided darkly. *Sightseeing* was the last item on his agenda.

'You must stay for dinner. I could ask Marc's parents to join us. After all, his father is your cousin. Have you never met?'

Don't, Emma almost cried out. It would be akin to setting a cat among the pigeons. Worse, for Nick Castelli was no ordinary cat—his affiliation to the feline family went beyond the domestic variety.

'When we were young, yes,' Nick concurred with a faint smile. 'Although I was barely in my teens when Bruno emigrated to Australia.'

'Then that's settled,' Mrs Templeton beamed, pleased with the prospect of what she envisaged would be a family reunion. 'I'll ring them at once. Shall we say six-thirty?'

'Thank you,' Nick responded gently. 'You're very kind.'

Kind? Emma didn't doubt the motive behind her mother's invitation. It was Nick's purpose that was highly suspect. And what was there to gain by causing Lena and Bruno Martinero the added pain of witnessing their son's widow in the company of another man?

Somehow Emma made it to the car, and once seated she waited only until they were mobile before accusing furiously, 'You did that on purpose, didn't you?'

The car reached the end of the street, then eased into the main stream of traffic heading towards the city.

She could feel herself begin to shake, both outwardly and inwardly, and she hugged her arms in an effort towards control, fixing her gaze beyond the windscreen and watching with mesmerised detachment the spots of rain that began to dot the plated glass. Within seconds they grew and spread as the elements lashed the car with windswept fury, restricting visibility to a minimum.

'Where are you taking me?' Even as she asked the question, she realised with startling clarity that he had only one destination in mind, and fear knotted her stomach into a painful ball. 'Damn you, Nick! *Damn you!*'

A muscle tensed along the edge of his jaw, and his eyes glittered with latent anger. 'Have a care, Emma. I'm not entirely familiar with this vehicle, or the precise route into the city.'

'Where in the city, exactly?'

'Adjacent Hyde Park.'

She directed him with cool civility and the minimum

of words, and it wasn't until he slid the car to a halt in the
entrance of an impressive hotel that she gave vent to her
anger.

'If you think I'm getting out of this car, you're
mistaken!'

'Brave words, *cara*,' he drawled with hateful cynicism.
'But you don't have a say in the matter.' Sliding out from
behind the wheel he crossed to her side and opened her
door, then leant forward and unfastened her seat-belt.

Emma became aware of the porter hovering discreetly
nearby, together with a uniformed attendant who
accepted the keys Nick handed him with polite
deference.

'Emma.' His voice held an invincible quality that
threatened retribution, but she was damned if she'd
meekly comply.

'Give me one valid reason *why*,' she sallied with
unaccustomed stubbornness, and saw his expression
harden into a compelling mask.

'You're coming with me, one way or another—so
choose, Emma,' he declared with bleak implacability.
'On your feet—or hoisted over my shoulder.' He paused
fractionally, then continued with deadly softness, 'I find
it difficult to believe you'd appreciate causing a
spectacle.'

She looked at him in silence for several seconds,
waging a mutinous war against his high-handedness.
However, capitulation seemed the only advisable course
if she was to retain a shred of dignity, and without a word
she slipped out from the passenger seat.

His hand closed round her arm with a steely grasp, and
she gritted her teeth together against his strength.

'You're hurting me.'

'Believe me, I'm showing remarkable restraint.'

They traversed the deep-piled carpeted foyer towards the elevator, and the doors whispered open within seconds of Nick pressing the call-button.

Inside, and mercifully alone in the confines of the electronic carriage, she turned to face him.

'What do you want from me?' It was a cry from the heart, and his features tautened until they resembled hewn stone.

'The truth.'

CHAPTER ELEVEN

'What *is* the truth, Nick?' Raw cynicism edged Emma's voice, lending it a mockery she'd never thought to possess.

The elevator slid to a halt and they emerged into an empty corridor. Nick indicated a door to the right, and when they reached it he produced a key, inserted it into the lock, then gently pushed her inside.

It was a suite, Emma discovered with a quick glance, and one commanding a top-of-the-range tariff, for the furnishings looked expensive and from this height there had to be a spectacular view over the harbour.

'Would you like a drink?'

Something seemed to snap inside her, and a burst of hysterical laughter emerged from her lips. 'Oh, by all means, let's observe the conventions.'

He crossed the lounge to a small bar-fridge and extracted two glasses into which he poured what appeared to be a fairly potent mixture of spirits before placing one glass into her nerveless hand.

'*Salute.*'

She took a generous sip and endeavoured not to cough as the fiery liquid hit the back of her throat. It tasted horrible, but it had the desired effect, for within seconds a delicious warmth invaded her veins, and she no longer felt quite so on edge.

'Now,' Nick began silkily. 'Suppose you explain why you fled so swiftly from the villa, and Rome.'

His voice was deceptively quiet, but his eyes were

dark, gleaming depths of inimical anger, and she began to shake, the tremors of her body seemingly beyond her control as she opted for flippancy. Anything else was madness.

'You don't mess around with the niceties, do you? Just aim for the jugular.'

She watched in mesmerised fascination as he replaced his glass on a nearby table, and there was everything predatory about his movements as he shortened the distance between them.

'I could easily have killed you when I telephoned the villa and discovered from my unusually flustered aunt that you had two hours previously boarded a flight out of Rome.' His voice hardened with frightening intensity. 'I returned at once, to find Annalisa distraught and confused. She quite wrongly attributed some of the blame for your exit on to her own head, imagining that you didn't want either of us and had consequently fled to avoid further embarrassment.'

Emma closed her eyes, then slowly opened them to find he was within touching distance, and she fixed her attention on the V of his jumper, unwilling to meet his gaze.

'I didn't mean for Annalisa to be hurt.' The words came out in a ragged flow of remorse.

'She wouldn't have been, if you had stayed,' Nick went on with pitiless disregard. His eyes darkened until they resembled polished onyx, glittery with unabated anger.

Emma took a backwards step as she glimpsed the icy rage apparent, and her eyes widened as he caught hold of her shoulders and dragged her close.

Even as his head lowered she twisted her own in a desperate attempt to avoid the forceful pressure of his mouth, and she gave an anguished groan as her lips were crushed with bruising insistence, his touch hard and merciless, almost cruel, as he sought the sweet inner moistness she fought so hard to deny him.

A shudder shook her slender frame, an almost convulsive reaction to the traitorous kindling of desire that swept like flame through her body, consuming all her inhibitions with galling swiftness.

Sheer perversity kept her mouth tightly closed, and it was only when his hand slid to capture her nape, his fingers tightening ruthlessly in the riot of curls there, pulling the tender roots, that she gasped against the excruciating pain. Then she almost cried as he gained entry, filling her mouth and plundering its depths with such utter devastation that it became nothing less than a total ravishment of her senses.

Nothing, *nothing* could be worse than this, she agonised mindlessly as she silently willed him to stop for fear she might slip into an engulfing, threatening void.

Then suddenly she was free, thrust roughly away, and she dimly registered his husky, almost guttural exclamation of self-disgust a few brief seconds before he pulled her back into his arms, burying her head into the curve of his shoulder, and she felt his lips drift softly against her temple.

'Forgive me,' he murmured gently. Fingers that seemed oddly shaky slid through her hair, and she felt a tremor run through his powerful body, heard the rapid thud of his heartbeat beneath her cheek racing almost as fast as her own; then his mouth travelled slowly to seek the sensitive curve of her neck, brushing the deep pulsing cord before lifting his hands to cup her face.

Emma closed her eyes against his dark, chiselled profile, and her mouth began to tremble of its own volition as his lips trailed over her cheekbones, the delicate length of her nose, then each closed eyelid in turn before claiming her mouth.

This time there was only gentleness in his touch, an incredible tenderness that was almost a benediction, as he traced the bruised outline with his tongue before sliding up to caress an earlobe, taking it gently between his teeth, and she could almost sense his smile as he murmured teasingly, 'Cara ... Bellissima. Or perhaps you would prefer amante—inamorata?'

Lover. Even thinking about those hours she'd spent in his arms brought a fresh flood of ignoble colour to her cheeks. Her voice seemed locked in her throat, unable to emerge, and after a few miserable seconds she let her lashes sweep slowly down, veiling their expressive depths.

'Emma?'

She not only couldn't speak, she couldn't bear to look at him.

'Dio,' Nick groaned emotively. 'How can you be so blind?' He shook her gently, and she felt his hands slip up to cradle her face. 'Look at me.'

Her eyelids quivered, then slowly flickered upwards in obedience, and she glimpsed the wealth of emotion apparent, the sheer depth of feeling that was solely for her.

'The past two weeks have been hell.' He lifted a hand and raked weary fingers through his hair, ruffling it into attractive disorder, and Emma glimpsed the tension etching his features, the bleakness evident in his eyes.

'I picked up the telephone at least once every night. There were so many words I wanted to say—simple, yet desperately important words, like—I love you. Instead, I was swayed by a pair of haunting gold eyes which alternately begged and pleaded with me, and I replaced the receiver before the call could connect.'

She wasn't capable of uttering so much as a word, and she watched with captivating fascination as Nick lifted a hand and brushed gentle fingers across her cheek, then along the edge of her chin, tilting it as he forced her to retain his gaze.

'I knew you needed time away from me, time in which to be able to evaluate your own feelings and gain some kind of perspective. I was sure of my emotions. Sure of yours.' A faint smile lifted the edges of his mouth, then twisted with a degree of cynicism. 'Does that sound presumptuous? God knows, I've suffered the tortures of the damned—wanting, needing you.' His expression became infinitely serious as he caressed the fine bones of her face. 'I want to be in your life, part of your future. I *know* I want you as my wife.' He paused, his eyes becoming deeply intent, and his hands slid down to her shoulders, his thumbs creating havoc as they moved absently back and forth along the delicate hollows at the edge of her collarbone. 'I want to kiss you until there isn't a vestige of doubt in your mind as to who I am. Hold you, *love* you. Never let you go.'

A shaft of exquisite longing began to unfurl deep inside her, radiating slowly until it encompassed her whole body.

'Marc——'

She lifted a hand and placed her fingers against his lips, silently begging him to listen, to understand what she had to say.

'Marc was——' she faltered slightly, searching for the right words. 'My very dear friend. It never occurred to either of us to question the quality of our emotions; we simply accepted our shared togetherness, the happiness we had, our mutual enjoyment of each other, and thought it was love.' Her mouth trembled a little, and her voice shook. 'Perhaps that's why I hated you so much,' she revealed with a trace of sadness. 'For showing me the difference.' Her eyes became wide and clear, almost luminous as she held his gaze. 'It made me afraid. Not only of you, but of myself.' Her fingers wavered as she felt his lips move, and she shook her head in silent negation.

'I imagined the warmth I shared with Marc was all there was to—sexual pleasure. Sensual ecstasy was something I believed to exist only in the imaginative female mind.' Her eyes roved over his features, seeing the rugged strength apparent, the depth of emotion evident, and gathered sufficient courage to continue.

'After that—night, with you, I felt like a traitor. To Marc, to myself.' A slightly hollow laugh emerged from her throat in a gesture of self-deprecation. 'I was filled with guilt in every conceivable form. And shock. Disbelief. All of those emotions. What was worse was being made painfully aware of a deep, abiding passion that daily became more impossible to ignore.'

Emma felt his mouth open beneath her fingers as he gently caressed each one in turn, then he removed her hand to thread his fingers through her own.

'So you ran away,' Nick declared softly, and she shivered beneath the latent sensuality evident in his eyes.

'I couldn't stay.'

'If I'd followed my baser instincts, I would have taken you to Milan with me and kept you chained to my side day and night,' he revealed with brooding, almost wry amusement. 'For most of that first week at the villa I had to content myself with being the ideal companion, convinced you preferred Annalisa's company to that of my own.' He slanted her a teasing smile. 'The only thing that gave me some hope was evidence of your increasing awareness of me, although I began to wonder if I would ever break through the silken threads of your self-made cocoon, and I was torn between using tender loving care and brute force. Fearful that if I lost control, I would merely succeed in frightening you with the strength of my desire. And you, my sweet Emma, were preoccupied with fighting your own inner battles. The result of which was a number of volatile clashes.'

His eyes darkened measurably for a few long seconds, then became vaguely rueful as he leaned his head down and bestowed a long, lingering kiss to her softly parted lips, deepening the caress with an evocative skill that stirred her senses and dispelled any lingering doubt.

Slowly she lifted her arms, linking her hands together behind his neck as she gave herself up to the elusive alchemy of his touch, and it was a long time before he slowly lifted his head.

Emma stood enraptured and totally bemused as he slid his hands from her waist up to close over her shoulders, helpless beneath an emotive maelstrom from which she never wanted to emerge.

'When will you marry me?'

She began to smile, a mischievous sparkle lightening her eyes to a brilliant shade of topaz. 'I wasn't aware I had been asked.'

She was lightly shaken for her temerity. 'Sweet fool,' Nick growled huskily. 'There can be no doubt that you *will*.'

Her expression sobered a little, her gaze becoming remarkably steady as she met the dark intensity apparent in his own, the latent passion evident, and she was aware of a matching aching need, a longing so tumultuous it was almost impossible to contain.

'A few months——'

'Next week,' he insisted with quiet certainty. 'I refuse to wait any longer.'

'You're joking!' The words left her lips in an incredulous gasp, and he shook his head, chiding gently,

'Don't make unnecessary obstacles, *cara*. Your need to be with me is almost equal to my own.'

'But we can't get married so soon' Emma declared shakily, her mind racing with a multitude of complexities.

'*Yes.* Believe it.'

She seemed momentarily lost for words, and he offered quietly, 'I want you with me, by my side every day and in my bed all night long.' His hands slid up to caress her face before slipping to cradle her head. 'To wake in the morning and see you there, *know* you are mine.' His voice was a soothing, slightly inflected drawl that carried the weight of his conviction. 'Could you live in Italy, do you think?'

It didn't matter where, as long as he was there, and she said so, her heart in her eyes. 'Yes. Milan—anywhere. Being together is all that matters.'

'*Grazie,*' Nick said gently. 'Annalisa will be ecstatic.'

'I will have to tell——'

'Your parents, Marc's,' he intervened quietly, 'will approve and agree when presented with a *fait accompli.* Be delighted for your future happiness with a man who regards you as the reason for his existence.' He paused, his eyes softening as he caught sight of her bemused confusion. 'There will be no difficulties, I promise.'

And there weren't. It was exactly as Nick had predicted, and Emma floated through the ensuing week on a euphoric cloud, finding it incredibly easy to fall in with every arrangement that was made.

The simple ceremony at the register office was quiet, with immediate family present, and afterwards there were only the closest of friends invited to a buffet dinner held in the privacy of her parents' home.

Hamilton Island, part of the Whitsunday group of islands in tropical North Queensland, had been chosen for a few days' holiday prior to their departure from Sydney for Rome. One of the more recently developed tourist resorts, Hamilton Island was advertised as an idyllic paradise, and it was exactly that.

Emma surveyed their luxurious unit with its panoramic view over the wide, sweeping pool to the sparkling blue ocean, then she turned back towards the man at her side.

'It's beautiful, so peaceful. Almost heaven,' she declared quietly.

'Almost, *amante*?' Nick teased huskily, pulling her close, and she looked up at him glimpsing the faint edge of tension beneath the surface, a waiting expectancy that was carefully hidden, yet there none the less.

Slowly, and with infinite care, she lifted her arms and linked them together at his nape.

'I love you,' she vowed simply. 'With everything I have to give—for as long as I live.'

His eyes flared with naked desire, then became dark with a deep, slumbrous warmth as he lowered his head down to hers, and she opened her mouth generously beneath the incredible gentleness of his own, glorying in his passivity as she initiated the kiss, exploring in a manner she would never have dreamt of doing in the past.

Fire swept through her veins, delicious and intoxicating, and she moved closer against him, exultant as she caught the faint, almost imperceptible catch in his breath before his mouth hardened, possessing hers with hunger and raw, aching need.

It was a long time before he reluctantly lifted his head, and the wealth of passionate intensity evident brought a faint tinge of delicate pink to her cheeks.

His smile was blatantly sensuous, the depths of his eyes filled with lazy amusement.

'What would you suggest, Emma Castelli?' he drawled softly. 'A stroll along the beach, a swim in the pool?'

She tilted her head to one side, contriving to give each suggestion some thought. 'You choose,' she offered demurely, and a soft, husky laugh left his throat.

'Such compliance.'

The temptation to tease him was irresistible. 'Perhaps we could explore the complex——'

'Witch! The only exploration I want to conduct is of *you*.' He trailed idle, almost chiding fingers along the edge of her jaw, then traced the outline of her mouth, his forefinger moving back and forth across the soft fullness of her lower lip in a gentle, caressing gesture.

An exquisite melting sensation consumed Emma's body, rendering her malleable, totally *his*.

'Do you need an invitation?' she whispered, becoming lost in the wealth of passion evident in his gaze, and without a word he swept an arm beneath her knees and lifted her into his arms, then he walked slowly towards the bedroom.

Part one in the gripping Savage saga.

When genteel Melody van der Veer is first deprived of her husband (and her home in England) by a jealous murderer and, subsequently, her freedom by American slave traders, she believes she has nothing else to lose.

But she is wrong. Soon she would lose all: heart, body and soul, to a fiery New Zealander and his war torn, windswept land.

An exciting new novel by popular author Hazel Smith.
Available January 1988. Price: £2.95

W❖RLDWIDE

Two lives, two destinies

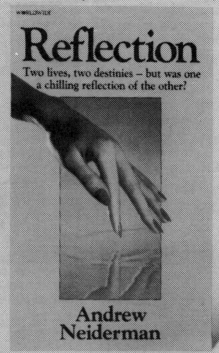

–but the same fate?

ACCEPT 4
MILLS & BOON
ROMANCES
ABSOLUTELY FREE

...after all, what better way to continue your enjoyment of the finest stories from the world's foremost romantic authors? This is a very special introductory offer designed for regular readers. Once you've read your four **free** books you can take out a subscription (although there's no obligation at all). Subscribers enjoy many special benefits and all these are described overleaf. ►►►

As a regular subscriber you'll enjoy

★ **SIX OF OUR NEWEST ROMANCES** – every month reserved at the printers and delivered direct to your door by Mills & Boon.

★ **NO COMMITMENT** – you are under no obligation and may cancel your subscription at any time.

★ **FREE POSTAGE AND PACKING** – unlike many other book clubs we pay all the extras.

★ **FREE REGULAR NEWSLETTER** – packed with exciting competitions, horoscopes, recipes and handicrafts... plus information on top Mills & Boon authors.

★ **SPECIAL OFFERS** – specially selected books and offers, exclusively for Mills & Boon subscribers.

★ **HELPFUL, FRIENDLY SERVICE** – from the ladies at Mills & Boon. You can call us any time on 01- 684 2141.

With personal service like this, and wonderful stories like the one you've just read, is it really any wonder that Mills & Boon is the most popular publisher of romantic fiction in the world?

This attractive white canvas tote bag, emblazoned with the Mills & Boon rose, is yours absolutely **FREE!**

Just fill in the coupon today and post to:
MILLS & BOON READER SERVICE, FREEPOST,
PO BOX 236, CROYDON, SURREY CR9 9EL.
